Festival in Therma

Peter G. Tripodes

Festival in Therma

by

Peter G. Tripodes

Los Angeles, California

Festival in Therma

Published in the USA by Birchwood Press

Los Angeles, California

Send inquires to: birchwoodpress@gmail.com

www.birchwoodpress.com

ISBN: 978-0-9965153-2-0

BIRCHWOOD
PRESS

Contents:

Origins

Encounters

Origins

Arethusa

Last night I dreamt of a dark plain which had once been ocean, and over it the shapes of my parents, now part of the night from which they had once sheltered me, each trying to be remembered, each repeating my name as if to summon me, one soft and lilting and carrying an expression of pleasure in expectation of beholding me, the other hard and deep and demanding an accounting.

My mother was born in 1908 on the Greek island of Ikaria in the village of Arethusa, named after a nymph who had fled the river god to preserve her chastity and transformed by the goddess Minerva into an underground stream to escape him, only to have his waters follow and finally merge with hers.

My mother died in 1990 in Pasadena of complications from a massive brain hemorrhage that had left her paralyzed and without speech, her eyes stabbing randomly at objects about her, uncoordinated and unfocussing, feeding back dizzy images to what remained of her brain. I had asked her to blink if she could hear me hoping she couldn't. She could. She blinked in the exaggerated manner of a child trying to show that it was not sleepy. I talked to her as to someone trapped underground who could never be brought back into the light, of how good she had been as a mother and of how I loved her, and of how terrible that this thing had happened to her. I wondered whether my words only pained her, forcing her to attend to matters in a world she could never again be a part of, interfering with her natural descent into death. I began to visit her less frequently, finally scarcely at all, and she died one afternoon when no one was there.

I had listened from childhood on as she and my aunt talked about Arethusa painstakingly assembling memories, filling in missing details for each other, patching and working and cross-comparing recollections, till they for that day fell into place as clear and vivid as their life in the America around them.

When my mother died, it left my aunt as the last who couldn't do it alone, and the whole thing came undone and with it my connection with their island origins.

I went to Arethusa to find them for my mother, who had been a loving and constant figure for me while she lived, but had become utterly mysterious to me after her death, reminding me of my childhood dream of her merging into the wallpaper across from my bed to return as a person unknown to me.

Ikaria is an island in the southern Aegean, too small to be shown on many maps and too undeveloped to draw many visitors there, the name deriving from the legend of Icarus, a youth who had ignored his father's warnings about flying too close to the sun which would melt the wax in his wings, and had fallen into the sea. I heard it again as a parable about origins and separation.

The island is a mass of mountains that forms a central spine along its length, wrenched by cataclysms and fissured by streams that run down its slopes to the sea on all sides. Small mountain villages lie nested within its folds, hidden from the view of pirates of earlier centuries, and largely unchanged to this day. Arethusa is one of them, high in the mountains and enshrouded in fog much of the year.

I had called ahead to Philip, an elderly cousin who lived there and who had known my mother as a child. I had not seen him since he had visited in America some years back and was surprised now that I had grown up to see how small he was. His wife Emily was small too, as was their house. They appeared like kindly elves in a children's story, delicate and softly mannered, vulnerable, yet strangely safe in this wild terrain. I bent my head down as I went through the door and entered a small green kitchen, which seemed to be the whole of the house and wondered if the furniture could hold me. I also wondered if in this tiny unreal place I could come to understand anything real about my mother.

Through the window I could see the giant face of a mountain, an awesome protective presence that helped keep

Arethusa hidden and inaccessible to sea pirates and other marauders. I fixed on it until I felt disoriented by its great mass and began to lose my sense of connection with anything here, as Philip softly reminisced his youth with my mother here, speaking of her in a manner I heard no other man ever speak, how beautiful she had been as a young girl running along these mountain pathways and I could tell that he had loved her, that she had gotten away and that he sought now to share his memories of her, but along a path that was his own.

Mine was of my mother as an old woman doing evening watering, standing waxen and still, worrying not to track wet into the house, separating outside from inside shoes, frozen in the image of her drying her hands by drawing them spread-fingered along her arms, age-softened, pink, and caring, her head tilted forward as if beckoning me to go on in and visit with my father, he a frozen figure, too, sitting at a table in his wheelchair, bibbed like an infant for feeding, yet maintaining an accustomed severity made neither more nor less by disease, and wondering what had become of me, if anything.

Childhood

I grew into my sixth year of childhood in the depression days of the early thirties on 154th and Kinsman on Cleveland's east side where we lived in a third-story tenement across from my father's restaurant, the Washington Lunch, whose name meant nothing to me then because we were Greek.

The restaurant was narrow, deep, and noisy, smelling of stale beer and squeezed between a small barber shop and an empty storefront with soaped-over windows. A long counter running along one side of it and ending at a kitchen door with a small diamond-shaped window from which the cook with a cigarette hanging from his lips could almost always be seen.

In the summer three small ceiling fans whirred with a noise that was the noise of summer and under it a veil of smoke and food smells that seemed never to move, which was all right with me, because I liked it, liked it because it meant I was safe here.

Safe even in the winter when drafts of freezing cold blew in whenever anyone came or left, bringing in the smell of dirty snow and people wearing two overcoats and coming in to beg for food, and my mother's warning to me to be careful because these people sometimes steal children like me and warning me also never to sit on the only toilet in the restaurant because, as she would moan darkly, it was used by "who else other than God knows who," which sounded doubly ominous in Greek.

Summer was my favorite when the noises were of people shouting and the screeching and clanging of streetcars stopping to let the conductors run in for a quick bite to eat, ordering something with a click of their fingers to get everyone moving, then eating faster than anyone else I had ever seen eat, and running back to drive their streetcars.

Our landlord, Mr. Toth, was one of them and had buttons pinned all around his black conductor's cap. Though he never smiled, he gave us buttons off his cap when he wasn't angry, and even let us watch him eat his dinner when Mrs. Toth said we could, when Mr. Toth felt good enough to have anyone like us watch him eat, when he'd let me and my sister stand on either side of his chair while he ate and let us listen for the clicking sound he made with his teeth, especially when biting into the boiled potatoes Mrs. Toth had cooked for him, letting us do all that without his ever saying a word, or even smiling. My sister and I would later try to make that same sound ourselves by clicking our teeth especially when eating potatoes but the sound never came out like his.

Things would die there, too, on Kinsman Avenue, mostly animals but also my friend Bobby, who was seven and had been run over by a truck while riding the Christmas wagon he had been waiting for forever, which made Kinsman Avenue forever a dangerous place to be, where my mother said I too could be killed, and never letting me forget it.

I had found out about Bobby getting killed that afternoon with my father rushing into the house and telling my mother, in a voice not meant for me to hear that Bobby had been crushed by a truck while riding on his Christmas wagon into Kinsman Avenue like my mother had always predicted he would, and said it using the Greek word *Yiosi*, which meant something more horrible than crushed, like something alive that had changed in a second to an unrecognizable stain in the street, an image of Bobby in death that stayed with me for years.

The second worst was Mr. Toth killing his two geese after having let my sister and me watch for a month while he fed them, stuffing food down their throats while they struggled to get free, which was also something I didn't need to see, nor wanted to see especially that day that he took them out, the two of them, then cutting their heads off with a knife while they wriggled to get free, something I didn't need my mother to tell me never to forget that too.

But inside the restaurant I was safe because my father was there and he wasn't afraid of anything until his own father died and he cried over it, which I didn't want to see because it made me feel less safe being with him.

My mother's father whom we called *Patera*, which meant father in Greek but was used for my grandfather too, would tell us stories whenever we visited him, all beginning with *Mia fora kai na kero*, which is "once upon a time" in Greek, which he would say with a hushed breath that floated around the room and held us, making us hungry for what would come next.

My father never thought *Patera* was very smart and would tell my mother what a fool her father was and, though whispered and not intended for us to hear, it was clear enough to me. Maybe it was because my father worked too hard to be able to think about things that weren't true, while *Patera* would talk only of such things and made us see the world as a magical place like he did. In the end my father came to feel that my mother was a fool too and expected that we would someday come to believe so too. But her way was magical like *Patera's* and, unlike my father's way, hers was a world in which one was never safe because things you didn't expect at all could come out of it and in a minute steal or kill you.

I don't know why I still needed my father's not believing anything that he couldn't see, and his expecting that I would do so too, for he could protect me while my mother could not and for that I loved him too, though in a way that I felt forever separated from him, as if he were a guard on duty, and for that he could have been someone else's father and not mine.

Peter G. Tripodes

Eye of the Beholder

atera, my grandfather, my mother's father, a soft and entertaining presence in life, now dead for some years, and newly remembered. His last name was Horaites derived, as he told it, from his ancestral village origins, the word for village in Ikarian dialect, Greek is *Xorio* and the word for villager being *Xoriatis*, transformed, again as he told it, to Horaites in English when he came to America, as something to be believed, which, with reservation, I did.

As it was with the Ikarian creation story he told in apparent seriousness to account for what he described as an undue fear and wariness found in many Ikarians, was that there was a point in time long ago when a woman fleeing for her life from Crete had come by some unknown means to Ikaria, which she believed to be uninhabited and, seeking shelter in a plot of tall grass, came upon a man similarly trembling for his life and hiding, then together, recovering from the initial terror of being discovered by the other, came to produce the first inhabitants on the island.

The distinction between legend and fact blurred in these tales, as in all his tellings and, since told without challenge, stayed in place for years.

I remember him, by contrast, as so different from the men on my father's side, all fiercely grounded in reality and none of whom respected *Patera*, evolving an atmosphere I grew up in, and one in which I came to side with him.

And to believe him as he related how he had been a very important and respected person in his village, Arethusa, having overseen the construction of *Ayia Marina*, the village church assembled of rocks and boulders from the mountainside as a tribute to deity and a monument attesting to the importance of those who had built it. As I saw it, in America, he found nothing to replace it with.

Religion on the island, particularly in mountain villages like Arethusa, merged with the concerns of daily life and assimilated into it in a kind of crude pantheism in which God and the Devil competed with each other and with humans in everything one saw or felt, and in which religion interfaced with an underworld of occult beings who darkly manipulated the fortunes of the living to cause them grief and in which God was beseeched to counter them through the burning of incense, which hovered everywhere.

Independently of my grandfather's creation tale, the origin of the island religion seemed pagan, an afterbirth that

Christianity in its more formal structure, could not begin to cast off and replace the dramatic and compelling account of occult mythic forces whose intricate machinations brought humans fully into play in the daily contest between good and evil, more compellingly than the dilute formal story of Christianity.

The mechanisms of the pagan world mysteriously issued from a cosmic design co-habited by both good and evil, each existing in equal force and presence, and equally involved in the affairs of humans.

The conduct of daily life was therein enacted as living theater, where human activity was determined by outside forces, caught in the contest for one's soul between God and the Devil. All one could do was avoid the evil eye as best one could, that targeted the hapless victim for the Devil to undo by someone's thoughtless praise of him.

My mother, my grandfather's first-born child and influenced strongly by him, pointedly sensed spirits about her all her life which were particularly active after my father's death that had widowed her, filling the otherwise empty rooms and left her with the leavings and signs of witches and angels about her, filling her waking hours and dreams.

My grandfather, at the end of his life, ritualizing his dying moments as theater, too, assembled his children and grandchildren, a dozen or more, to a makeshift bed set up in his living room as he lay dying, palpably exiting life before our eyes, beckoning each of us in turn to his bedside to look for him after our own deaths. When my turn as the first-born grandchild came to sit by his side, he held his arms up as if to the heavens, as if in prayer for me, then slowly lowered and rested them on my shoulders, pulling me forward to rub his coarse beard stubble along my cheek, and rasp in my ear, *Petrakie, tha se pothemeso, Petrakie* being an endearing diminutive term for Peter ordinarily reserved for children younger than me. He was saying, "I shall miss you," uttered as if, on my arrival to that other life, he would be waiting for me.

I took a trip to Arethusa long after everyone to whom it might have been important to have gone there with me had died, and found myself unaccountably grieving that they were not there to share their better years with me, to show me what they had left behind.

Everything in Arethusa seemed as unreal to me as my grandfather's stories of it, as if the village had been drained of the life that once had been there, far less real in my visiting than had been in their telling. The houses, scarcely more than stone and plaster huts, appeared as if in miniature, like a doll-house recreation of what they had described as having left, tiny houses strewn over rocky slopes, some crumbling back into the earth, their inhabitants tiny woodland creatures, fairy tale versions of what I had expected, and the church my grandfather had made so much of appeared to me small and crudely built, much more in my grandfather's eyes than it appeared to me.

Upon leaving I found myself oddly nostalgic for I knew not what.

Peter G. Tripodes

Birthday Shoes

I t was for my fourteenth birthday. A pair of shoes.

My only thought was that I didn't want any. For one thing, they would hurt, and, for another, I already had a pair. And for a third, I didn't like Mr. Kotis anyway, who was coming over on my birthday to sell my mother a new pair of shoes for me. I knew how he'd be telling her, "Got some right here that are perfect for the boy," which was never true.

The whole family was here, which wasn't really about my birthday. They would be here anyway because they were always here on Sundays: my aunts, uncles, cousins, everyone. Getting together on Sunday after church was a custom my parents brought from Greece. With a family as big as ours, it was always someone's birthday, which made mine not very special anyway.

The difference today was Mr. Kotis. He wasn't normally invited to family Sundays. He wasn't part of the family and he would be here simply to sell shoes. It was embarrassing, his doing that in front of everyone.

Mr. Kotis sold shoes out of a small shoe case, sold them from door to door and at gatherings like this one when he could get someone to invite him. If he knew that he was here mostly because my mother felt sorry for him, he didn't let on. Not one bit. He carried himself like he was important, like we were all here especially for him. When my mother first told me he'd be coming here to show me some birthday shoes, I didn't like it. Not only that: I knew he'd be trying to sell everybody he could get to buy a pair of shoes. It was embarrassing.

Mr. Kotis's shoe case. I remember it from before. A few pairs of shoes in it that he used as samples to show how good the shoes he was selling were, and his spiral book of photographs of other shoes.

The first thing Mr. Kotis did after introductions was to draw up a chair in the middle of the kitchen, sit me down in it, beckon those who would listen to form a close circle around us, then proceed to show the photos in his book, one of which he said I could choose. Of course, only the women came into the kitchen to hear him. The men didn't like Mr. Kotis and stayed in the living room. If Mr. Kotis was aware of how the men felt about him, he didn't let on. He sat with his head high and his back straight in a chair next to me and nodded like an actor to acknowledge the women in the kitchen who had come in to see.

After waiting to be sure he had everyone's attention, he took a deep breath, took a deep breath, pulled back the sleeves of his suit jacket over his cufflinks and reached into his shoe case. In the manner of a magician about to perform a trick, he brought out a business card, flipped it around several times as if to show nothing was hidden, and began to read aloud from it: "Nicholas J. Kotis, Trust me to find the perfect shoe for you." Then held the card high over his head for everyone to see.

He reached into the shoe case again and brought out two pairs of sample shoes, not of my size but samples of what he could get for me, waved them one after the other in the air, then returned them to his shoe case. "There is quality in these," he said, tapping the sides of the shoe case once he had settled the sample shoes in it, "and now I have these also for you to see." He reached in again and brought out his spiral book of photographs of shoes. Before opening it, he held it high so that everyone could see, then brought it down, placed it on his lap, and opened it, slowly turning one page, then another, each time first holding it up for viewing, then reading aloud what was written there. He read every word very slowly and carefully so as not to mispronounce anything. Every now and then, if the shoes on a page showed a picture of a boy wearing them, he'd point to me and say, "Don't you think this boy here would also look good in these?" Some of the women would take the opportunity to say something to my mother, like "Those are the ones, I think, for him. Very sturdy for active feet. You should get him those." Occasionally the women would argue among themselves in hushed tones, until Mr. Kotis raised his hand to quiet them.

Mr. Kotis was very proud of having gone through high school in America and worked hard at showing it. It was that, I think, that made the men in my family dislike him all the more. None of them had gone through high school in America or even in Greece and did not speak English as well as Mr. Kotis did, so they sat in the other room and smoked. It didn't help either that their women thought Mr. Kotis to have a certain sophistication that their own men, keeping more to the ways of the old country, didn't have.

I finally turned to him: "Mr. Kotis," I said, "I don't want any shoes."

He took a deep breath, smiled so that everyone could see that he was undismayed and then in a loud voice that everyone could hear, even the men in the other room, "You haven't even looked at them, my boy. There are some wonderful shoes here, indeed there are. Let's look again." He opened his book of photographs again, flattened his hand over each page, resting it there before turning it, and reading again what was written under it.

"I don't want any," I said, standing up, looking to my mother to see if it was all right for me to leave, maybe go and sit with the men in the other room.

She shook her head and motioned me to sit down again.

"Look at this boy's shoes." Mr. Kotis sighed as I sat down again. He motioned me to hold up my foot. "No, the other one," he said, pointing to the shoe with broken laces.

"Someone get this boy's father to come over here and tell me that this boy doesn't need a pair of shoes."

Mr. Kotis didn't mean it, of course, getting my father to come in, because my father never would have anything to do with him and, least of all, get in the middle of Mr. Kotis's trying to sell me a pair of shoes. His calling for my father was just to pressure me because my father didn't like him either, not one bit, which Mr. Kotis must have known too. Besides, my father might have resented my being the reason for his being called in.

Part of the problem was Mr. Kotis's manner, which my father described as "pretending to be a big shot," which immigrants like my father regarded as a pose to mask their origins.

But the real problem was Mr. Kotis's appearance. For one thing, my father and uncles were on the short stocky side and wore their hair high and wavy on their heads in the style of Greek immigrants of the time, whereas Mr. Kotis was tall, lean, with a high forehead and thinning hair cut close. For another, the men in my family always wore the same clothes home that they worked in at their restaurants, smelling of cooking oils and tobacco, while Mr. Kotis always dressed in a tie and business suit and with the slightest scent of cologne."He was showy," my father said, "dressing and smelling like that, like Woodland Avenue *marvri* on a Saturday night." Woodland Avenue, the black ghetto in Cleveland at the time. What my father was saying about Mr. Kotis was the worst thing he could say without out-and-out insulting him.

We'd heard the story more than once about how Mr. Kotis got reduced to selling shoes by borrowing money to open his own restaurant and going bankrupt because he wouldn't do anything but stand at the door in a white dinner jacket waiting for customers to come in. "Didn't have a pot to piss in," my father said, "and his carrying on like a big shot manager. That is what I would say is a fool."

I remember the photograph in our family album of Mr. Kotis in his restaurant posing like an actor before a large potted fern by the cash register in his white dinner jacket. He was everything that the men in my family didn't like in a man and used him, as an example of what none of us should ever become.

Yet, as I saw him—Mr. Kotis had a certain dignity, even a majesty about him, a theatrical and lofty presence, within which he could create any situation, any enactment of his choosing, something the men in my family had no inclination to.

One Sunday afternoon, years later, my parents had invited Mr. Kotis, his wife, Artemis, and his son Leo, who was about my age, to come to the family house for dinner to celebrate my just having gotten a graduate degree. It was my mother's idea, and she had arranged it so that Mr. Kotis could see what a fine young man she had raised. It was also for her to see Mrs. Kotis, Artemis, again, who had been the one who introduced my parents to each other many years earlier and so was forever romantically ingrained in my mother's mind as someone who had helped start our family and somehow who therefore had a stake in what had evolved from it, such as my getting a graduate degree.

My father's view of Mr. Kotis, who came dressed as usual in a suit and tie and a manner to match, was not softened by that circumstance and continued to regard Mr. Kotis as a fool whom he had again to endure.

My father also tended to regard Mr. Kotis's son, Leo, in the same way, viewing him distastefully as more like his father than not. Leo had come nattily dressed and pointedly urbane—all of which my father regarded as Leo's being without substance, as someone playing the big shot in the manner of his father and especially because he did not have a real job, working sporadically as a singing waiter in Italian restaurants in and around Hollywood.

I saw Leo quite differently, as someone having his father's gift for presentation and theater, which I appreciated, as my mother did, while my father also looked pained with the prospect of enduring him.

Neither father nor son disappointed my father's grim expectations, for in the middle of dinner, Mr. Kotis stood up and proposed a toast congratulating me for my degree, which went on for several minutes, at the end of which he suggested that his son Leo sing a song befitting the occasion while the rest of us ate. Unaccountably, Leo chose to sing a Dean Martin cabaret-style version of "Volare—an Evening in Roma," which was probably part of his professional repertoire and somehow judged by him appropriate to the occasion.

I watched my father wincing throughout, probably noting that the reference to Roma didn't sound Greek to him or even relevant to anything else of the evening. I followed him with my eyes as he pushed himself back from the table, stood up and left the room.

It was one of the few times I could share my father's world with him.

Father's Day Visit

My father, the one we relied on for everything but love, which he couldn't give, my mother shriveled almost to death for want of it until he became crippled and weak and human and reached out only then, so trembling in his need that it was almost unbearable.

My mother, who presided over his decline with bitterness and resolve, unable to cheer him or get herself to try, taking comfort only in the irony that she, the weaker of the two, was the one left standing, left to protect and suckle him, someone who had never been her own.

Coming to visit him on this Father's Day, I stood at the door of the house, an entry-way known so long to me yet unfamiliar now, shielded by my mother's camellia bush planted years before, her own plant that she would not allow trimmed or cut down, that had grown wild and high, now scratching at the door with the wind, sensing the dying monster refuged here who had grown weak as it had grown strong, she fed it as my father starved, and it sought now to enter here with me.

And so I went, though mostly for her, for my mother, to dilute her being here alone with him. He was in her care, continuously, when she no longer loved him, someone who could not love him, who had been cheated by him and who couldn't leave him, ever and especially now, she presided over his decline with bitterness and resolve comforted only by her martyrdom, by her having taken care of someone for so long who had never loved her, and by the irony that she, the weaker, had been left standing after the stronger had been felled and that he was now with her at last, needing her to protect him, and would have clawed himself free had he but the strength to leave. And even with that she spoke still of how his hair had been the softest she had ever touched, how she could not believe its softness when she had first touched it, how it came to promise a softness she found thereafter not to be in him, even now using that memory to soften this time, to see herself as giving care to a dying man who once had the softest hair she had ever touched.

On this Father's day, my mother's footsteps as they had always been, slippered sounds soft and quickening as she came to open the door and smile full to the brim with unabashed pleasure in seeing me, an island of good feeling, as familiar and warm as old cloth, greeting me as always, "Hello honee,"slightly falsettoed and rising at the end on the drawn out "ee," a special child-like squeal she used for little children and for me, it told me how I was for her, loved as always, then my asking, "How are you Ma?" and her sighing and making the sign of the cross, a self-parody long familiar to me and done now to tell me that nothing had changed, as she beckoned me in.

"He's in the kitchen," my mother said. Yes, that's where he would be, in the kitchen, a symbolic place, the meeting place of the healthy, where my father had in earlier days met visitors on at least equal terms and who ate his food at his table, at the table of the master of this house then thick-limbed and strong. Only not now. No longer. I went in and found the table bare, my father sitting shriveled in his wheelchair at his old place at the table, facing the window, his back to me, as if preparing to be alone, now and forever, hands together palm in palm resting on the table edge. I stood behind him for an instant, as behind a stranger, letting him go out of focus and then back in again.

The idea for my coming on this Father's Day, I think my mother's, certainly not his nor mine, was to have us have a time to talk, just him and me, on this last Father's Day as we expected it to be, her gift to him through me, her last, presenting him with his son again.

He would not have asked this, to be visited on his special day, a holiday, which he disliked, these inventions of merchants, his words, those, and they had, over time, settled also on me, for I was his son and thought in some ways as he.

I took a seat across from him, facing him, folding my hands together palm in palm and resting them on the table edge to reflect his, completing the symmetry, postured in ceremonial opposition, toy seated soldiers stamped from the same die and then turned to face each other. I fell into this design without thought, shaping my way to his, the child copying his father, as when a child I did his walk and tilt of his head till they settled in and became my own. Aged warriors now making peace. Nothing left to save here, though, silent and bare here, nothing to say here, only to finish and leave.

As my mother left the room, he turned slowly to face me and I said, "You're looking better," to no point for he looked terrible and knew it. He raised his eyes to look at me. Not a happy look, but a mask-like look that made me feel cold. He stayed that way for some seconds until his face softened, almost imperceptibly, but I knew that slight softening look, not much in itself but a lot in him, unusual enough to be remembered. "Glad you came," he said, then turned his palms upward as if feeling for rain, as if preparing to receive something from above or from me, from somewhere, something to fall into his hands, something to be placed there, something to close his fingers around and take back to his bed.

"I'm glad I came, too, Pa," I said, just to say something, then watched him put his hands together and look down at them. If there was something on his mind, he would come to it his way.

I knew that about him too. For he had a rhetorical way about him, always had, a kind of indirection, a way of control, grown even more pronounced in old age, a way of pausing and waiting, taking time to shape things to his will. "You know what?" he said, turning to look away, to look out the window, as if at something distant while preparing his words, then, looking back down at his hands, said, "Your mother is always angry at me," then paused and added, "You know what she said this morning?" He stopped right there, like that. He was getting to where he wanted to go. He waited for me again. "What?" I asked. "She said I never wanted to be with you when you were little, when you needed me to."

My mother must have heard him for she came in to ask what we were we talking about. "Nothing in particular," I said, then looked to my father, sitting still as stone, looking out the window, away from us. Without turning to face me, he said, almost plaintively, "You know, you could wheel me outside for a few minutes. I'd like to see the yard. Nobody takes me out there anymore."

Still looking out the window and his back still to me, he repeated, "Could you wheel me outside? I'd like to see the yard. Nobody takes me out there anymore."

I backed his wheelchair out of the kitchen and pushed it ahead of me toward the front door. He had a ramp built there some years earlier but did not use it often. It seemed my mother wouldn't take him out anymore, so no one did. She now opened the front door for us.

The camellia bush has spread out over the doorway and part-way onto the ramp, and I had to maneuver to get his wheelchair around it. My father seemed afraid of it as if it were a menace he had forgotten about that now challenged him. He was angry, like I remembered him from childhood, revitalized by this adversary, growling under his breath, "That goddam thing."

It was difficult for me to get the wheelchair around it and still keep on the ramp. He was leaning over to one side to keep the branches out of his face, but the bush seemed to be everywhere and managed to get entangled in one of the wheels. I pulled the wheelchair back and forth to get it free, but one wheel was caught solid. "Listen, Pa, I'm going inside for a garden clippers to cut your wheel loose." I left him cursing at the bush under his breath. It took me a few minutes to locate the clippers and by the time I had gotten outside again my father was in awful shape. He had apparently tried to pull the branch off the wheel by himself and, in his agitation, had tilted the wheelchair well into the bush. I righted the wheelchair and pulled the camellia branches from around his face. He looked disoriented and I became concerned. He had gotten scratched over his arms and elbows in his attempts to get free and looked wild, like he didn't know just what had happened. "Get me inside," he whispered. All the life was drained from him and he was trembling. My mother came out to help me and between the two of us we carried him to his bed. I went back to free the wheelchair and when I returned to his room to wish him a happy Father's Day, he was already asleep. My mother walked me to the front door and said, "I guess that's all he could take today."

That night I dreamt of my father and of me as a mix of me as a child and as I am now. The place was the noisy streets of my Cleveland childhood, screeching with iron streetcars and hurried with strangers. My father was trying to get home from where he had been treated that day for being a cripple, hurting and wanting to go home but his wheelchair was broken with one wheel half off and so I went there to help him get home, pulling and dragging him and the wheelchair and then I lost them both, like dogs suddenly no longer at my side. He got away from me I'm not sure how with that wheelchair broken like that, lost there now on a big street that could kill him. It was on that same street that I had first seen something die—a horse pulling a cart that made a horrible sound on a hot day like this, stumble, fall forward and become dead with a shudder that made its sweat fly off. I knew my father was around here somewhere trying to get home crawling and pulling that wheelchair and its crooked wheel trying to get it all home.

And then there he was lying in a little field filled with cans and bottles and papers blown there by the wind and caught by the weeds, dirty sticky summer weeds that grew in the cracks and dirt in Cleveland everywhere. He was lying there his body in those weeds and his head propped up in that heat against a brick wall asking me to find him his wheelchair, that it was somewhere in that field, and that I should look for it. Everything there looked like his wheelchair but wasn't. Old desk chairs and strollers and wagons, lots of things with wheels, all broken, and then there it was in the middle of the field, fallen sideways and part-way under the weeds like they were tearing at it trying to eat it. I pulled at it but couldn't get it free.

I went back to where my father had been by the wall but he had crawled away from there. I asked if anybody had seen him, an old crippled man crawling through and around here and trying to get home. Yes, he might be cut up some now from the broken glass where he had been lying because his wheelchair was broken and he had been crawling like this on his elbows and did they see him?

No. They had not. I found him only later, much later that day, farther down the street, streaked with dirt and looking very tired. How he had gotten there I don't know but I found him and he was grateful to me for it. I picked him up in my arms and carried him home. He asked me about his old wheelchair and felt badly that it was lost and asked what could be done. I didn't know what to tell him and then saw that he had fallen asleep and carried him home.

Looking for Andy

A ndy was the oldest man I had ever up till that time seen,
lots older than my grandfathers even, nearing a hundred
as it was told to me, born a slave who never learned to read
and wasn't himself sure how old he was—my mother said old
Andy might be a hundred, an ancient cave creature now
living in the cellar of my father's restaurant—living in what was
to me the bowels of the earth, Andy himself seeming a part of it, a
part of the earth, and slow moving, sometimes barely moving,
sometimes not moving, and all with effort, but grinning all the
time when you'd look at him, grinning from the corners of that
cellar if he sensed anyone else down there, grinning like a slave
finally got to be free, who'd wandered from city to city to end up
here, in a cellar in Cleveland, to carry sacks up to the kitchen for
my father and in return be allowed to live down there and
come up for food when he'd need to.

A gesture of kindness in those Depression days from my
father who let him live down there. It doesn't seem like much

now, but I suppose that then it was.

In return, Andy would bring up from the cellar whatever he was asked to bring, sometimes heavy bags that labored him, carrying them slowly up the cellar steps, breathing hard and resting at each, slowly like a mule over a known path.

"Why can't you let me help him, Papa?"

"Because Andy wouldn't want you to."

And no one much looking at him when he moved, no more than you would at your own shadow. He was used to that, to no one much looking at him. When he'd catch me looking his way too long, looking at the creases in his skin, gray powdery creases, like he'd been dipped into gray breading and rubbed till the black skin showed shiny through, looking like an unfinished statue, waiting for the human part to be finished in, he'd notice me looking. And grin me his aboriginal grin, as if in appreciation and he'd say—always the same thing: "I got twenny-one chillen like you," and if I kept looking at him, "Twenny-one of 'em," he'd say, "They're somewhere, sure, somewhere, sure," his voice trailing off and letting his grin fall away, his big lips barely moving behind his words, no extra breath behind them at all, telling me—by saying that—that he'd come from somewhere, that someone would have to know when he died, that someone should look for at least one of his children when he died and tell them their daddy was dead, find maybe one that would want to know what had happened to him.

The cellar was used for storage, with bags of rice and potatoes and onions and boxes of old dishes and cutlery, and in a corner had a changing room with a toilet, hardly big enough to turn around in.

Looking for Andy in the dark, I'd listen for his snoring to tell where he was, to wake him up to do something, and always worried when I couldn't hear him, worried that he was dead, that what was already so close had finally caught up with him.

And worried that I'd go down there one time and yell into the darkness, "Andy, my pa wants a bag of onions!" and nothing would come back but the wind and I would know that Andy was dead, and none of his kids the wiser for it.

I didn't really have to be told. I knew it was around him, that Death was around Andy all the time, that it was down there in the cellar with him, that it watched him in his sleep, watched him move more slowly all the time, watched him trudge up the stairs carrying a burden too heavy for him, harder and harder for him to make it all the way up, stopping to catch his breath, then getting to the top, and grinning. It was watching in silence and counting out Andy's last.

The wind blew out of the cellar and the dust billowed up like it had been centuries since the place had been cleaned out.

Old Andy's remains must still be there. I couldn't remember when he'd died. Or any of his kids being told. Or anything.

Isle of Capri

M y mother's off-key singing in the kitchen of "The Isle of Capri," not in self parody but pulsed inward to night flower scents and tango sweeps, to girlhood dreams recalled, beyond my father's incapacity for magic in a woman's way, and beyond us, too, her children who kept her earthbound.

Asimina, her sister, the only one to whom she ever fully revealed herself, an old photograph of the two taken when young women in Greece, taken years after their mother's death, the two standing together in continuing melancholy, dressed in black, Asimina's head on my mother's shoulder and my mother's head tilted on hers, their arms braided sisterly, their somber faces fixed forever in memory of their having awakened together one morning then as children to find their mother dead, so bonded till their deaths in the thought of that.

I had long heard the tale of her own mother's death but never fully sensed her abiding guilt, which seemed to rise in her every recollection of childhood, not until a holiday dinner when she, seated at one end of the table, aged, ill, and bent, my father in a wheelchair at the other end, my wife and children, my brother and his sprinkled along on either side, talking, eating, our attention diffuse, my mother reminiscing about childhood days in her village in Greece, about precipitous mountain trails that were rocky and steep, difficult to walk at night. I'd heard parts of this before, not important enough to follow while listening also to my father and others talking at the same time of other things to pick up a word here and there, to follow what they were saying too, each speaking to all, scattered humming dinner talk—that suddenly stopped when we heard my mother sob with an intensity that I had never heard before, what had she been saying? I reached over and put my hand on hers as she, in a child's breathless broken talk, recounted the story that we all knew, about her having gone on foot to an apothecary to get medicine for her mother, taking hours to get there and back with two small bottles of medicine, the rain having washed the labels clean, she might have guessed wrong which was which and condemned forever never to be sure as in that morning when she and her sister found their mother dead.

Her father remarried, my mother taking her new mother as a penance, a burden to be endured. "We must love her," my mother would say to us children, "she has taken my own mother's place."

But neither my mother nor Asmina ever found the new mother a replacement for the old, and they mourned the old one each day fresh, never taking the new one as their own.

Inevitably taking then my mother's part, I also saw the new one as not one of our own but a harsh surrogate I didn't really know, so unlike my mother or Asimina, who were loving, caretaking women, ever at ease with us, which this new one, harsh and carping, was not. "How come she's like that, Ma?"

We called her *Mitera,* which means mother more than grandmother in Greek, but sometimes goes over to grandmothers as a fonding term, ironic here, as we inherited from my mother the feeling that this grandmother was not one of our own.

And to assure her that she was, my mother would take my sister, brother, and me as children to stay with her in *Mitera's* cold-water flat in Chicago, its small dungeon-like rooms souring under the smell of urine and mold, where we listened at night to screams from the street and watched by day *Mitera* struggling to scrub her little burrow clean, closing it against the world. I wondered how *Mitera* and my grandfather had gotten so poor as to end up in this awful place and I would ask my mother, "When are we going home, Ma?"

As if angry at having been bargained into a place from which she could not escape, and having no children of her own, *Mitera* took out her ill will on my sister, brother, and me, not like a mother or grandmother but like a witch among us, not one of us at all, and I would ask my mother, "Why is she like that, Ma?"

And the reason that was told was that part of *Mitera's* life had been lived in another world, one with no connection to this one, the memory of which still haunted her.

The link between Mitera's two worlds was a photograph on her dresser of a woman, stern, unloving, and severe, who looked like *Mitera* to me. "Is that *Mitera's* mother?" I would ask. "No," my mother would say, "that's the princess who used to take care of her when she was young like you."

"She doesn't look like a princess, Ma."

And in bits and pieces, we were told how *Mitera* had loved the princess who had been like a mother to her, who had taken a fancy to her and taken her in when she was only twelve, when her own mother had to give her up, that she then lived in the palace for twenty-three more years. "Then why does she live here, Ma? Why does she now live like this?"

Mitera would from time to time talk of it, and when I asked her to tell me more, she would start to fill in some missing part, then struggle as if for breath and, after a few words, stop till asked again.

There had been great poverty in Ikaria in the 1880s when *Mitera* was a child and her mother had to give her up because she could no longer feed her. *Mitera,* one of six children, all of whom had been given up to others who could take care of them, and only one of whom she would ever see again.

And *Mitera* would tell how she had been taken from her mother by her aunt who worked as a seamstress at the palace of a Sultan in Constantinople, in the court of his daughter, Princess Fatima Mehmet, taken by boat through the strait of Dardanelles and the Sea of Marmara to the sultan's palace, the aunt perhaps intending to have her work with her. *Mitera* was said to have been at that time doll-like, delicate and fragile, with soft brown hair that went down to her feet, much like the delicate Circassian girls who were favorites in the harem, and that Princess Fatima took *Mitera* to keep at her side, to keep her chaste as we were led to believe, an exotic toy. She molded *Mitera's* loyalty to her taste and groomed her to become one of the most trusted of her servants, the Keeper of the Key, Custodian of the Treasury, which she became at seventeen and stayed till the Princess died, the Sultanate dissolved and Kamel Ataturk came to power.

And she described the end of those days as terrible, the princess dead, everyone including herself at peril, fleeing the palace in disarray, she recalled the flight of the palace dwarfs running about in terror holding their heads. She went back to the island and to her old village penniless, which was when my grandfather met her and began the life, which we later came to see.

Festival at Therma

M y brother had always been much into the family and had always lamented, I felt, that I had not. But I couldn't avoid the feeling as long as I could remember of not being able to stand for one more minute the intense blandness of being there.

And so I left but not without wanting to be one of them. They had brought something from the Greek island from which they came that had never been transmitted to me and without which I had always felt unprotected. That something was the abiding sense of being at one with one's culture, of being surrounded by and resonated to by beings like oneself, inter-permeated with them and so fortified that one was complete, and so able to rock endlessly in place like the old men who sat in curbside chairs in those island villages for the whole day doing nothing, like dogs in the sun. They had brought that here with them and saw only each other and practiced that oneness among themselves, my brother among them. Not having that sense, I felt that nothing was happening and found the quiet crushing.

After the death of my parents and the subsequent sale of our family house, my brother called to tell me my check was ready and would I like to have lunch with him, just us brothers. He had been almost killed in a freak accident at the Westwood Marquis parking garage a year earlier and had since been consumed with the celebration of his survival. With a gambler's optimism he took the near-tragedy as an omen, an unmistakable sign that he was intended to live, and even more, that he was intended to live well, and he went out and bought a new car and some new clothes.

He was loud and flamboyant and loving, with the flooding cadenced exuberance of a preacher, and as true as anyone I have ever known. I loved him too, though confusedly, not because of his exaggerated manner, which I found refreshing in that household, but because he had also been my rival for my mother's love, and yet one so loving that he forced me to do battle not with him but with myself, and I pushed away from him to avoid it. His eyes were the color of an amulet given me at my birth to ward off the evil eye, a blue that turned out to be prophetic for as we grew up it became clear to me that he would try to save me from separating myself into exile, and failing that he would do the next best thing, which was to become my good self, my surrogate who would carry but never wear the eldest son's mantle that I was to abandon, who was later to become the self who took on the care of my parents and who after their deaths walked the rooms of that empty house until his grief wore out.

Everything about him was explicit and literal. And he was not different in his mourning. He would murmur their names when he was in that house to announce that he was near, intending to reassure them by his soft presence as one would a child afraid of the dark, they now the children in their yet unaccustomed deathly place, and he comforted them as they had once him. He sensed them about him as palpable presences, and took me along with him to share in this meeting, encouraging me to talk to them too. Though I could not share his sense that they were really there, I went along with it as best I could, fearing that I would find myself false at every step. It was compelling yet senseless, like our choice of waterproof caskets to protect their bodies as a final caretaking, and I saw all my studied apprehensions about the dark being brightly resolved into a child's nursery tale about how things are. And I did talk too, as if to them, though too quietly to have him or even myself hear, embarrassed and awkward and feeling false, the symbol pretending to reality and seeking to be bonded and confused with it. I tried to muffle the deception by only thinking their names rather than speaking them. But my brother in his pure and guileless way intended this not as a symbolic communion but as a real one and called to the spirits of my parents with pointed clarity, intending fully to get their attention. I became ashamed that I almost felt that his doing this was in part to groom me as as his new parent, to regain through me what he had lost of them, and I half expected that I would next hear him announce to them in a clear voice that I had indeed undertaken to do so and that all was well and he was no longer an orphan, as if forcing that engagement by his announcement.

Thus I was in these ways the opposite of him and felt corrupt, accepting nothing in its easiest light, full of cynicism and bile, envious and untrusting. I had long connived to win my mother for myself but then lost out in her last days when only he could bear to be at her side in her grotesque death agonies, sharing prayer book readings with her, which I could not. He had, in her last light, overtaken me with that secret communion, preparing himself and her for her soul's exit, while I stayed elsewhere, preparing to ask how she was and was she still alive.

At lunch we talked about our parents' death, the sale of the house, and the shortness of life. The conversation seemed dreamlike as I looked at him across the table and could see only the child, the youngest of us, whom my mother had dressed in a pale yellow hand-me-down smock one morning that made him look like a little girl in this, my sister's dress, really too big for him, alternately tucked here and ballooning there, a memory that always stayed with me.

My feeling was that of being in an unknown place and

listening to someone I had known elsewhere sitting across from me, hearing his voice as of that child, speaking to me now as brother to brother and my not being able to hear him in a clear way.

When we got back to his car he played a CD of a Greek song from the islands sung by an old man in a distant sobbing wail so familiar in island songs, but sounding freshly poignant now. The song was about celebrating life by dancing wildly atop the earth before it draws you in and not to fear for your shoes for they will have time enough to rest after you are gone.

He played it, I think, to invite me to reflect with him on our lives, the memory of our parents and on the island heritage that bound all of us. The song took me to thoughts more my own, to a festival I had gone to in Therma, a village on the southern coast of Ikaria, the Aegean island where our parents were born. I had gone there to trace their paths through the villages they had talked about, to find after their deaths some belated sense of connections, and watched there an old man, frail and stubble-bearded, dance sweat-soaked by himself for hours to a song much like this one, who danced with creaky grace, gingerly turning and bending over cricket legs, arms held up and angled out at the elbows like bat wings, moving haltingly through less than their accustomed space.

The dance itself was made to the manner of aged limbs, its strokes and moves meant to be measured, understated, and held pensively in place before being deftly settled an inch to the left or right, as subtle as a magician's finger touch, impossible to track on first seeing. It was a cobra's dance, accompanied by a song that was a cry out of a mountain canyon, curved and modulated by its walls, a wail without distinguishable words, a sigh squeezed through the throat to sound out a high-pitched lamentation whose wordless meaning was, Oh God, it has come to this. It was more Turkish than Greek, more Muslim than Christian, and betrayed in wordless sound those strains of the island's diverse ancestry that the dance itself encoded.

I began to feel in it a terrible sadness, that it was not a celebration of life but of loss, of the dissolution of culture and the emergence of mongrel forms, the wail that of a bastard weeping to be reunited with its origins.

Most of the people at the festival were from Therma or nearby villages, like Agios Kirikos, where I was staying and which, like Therma, is edged to the sea by a wall of mountains that merged this night black with the sky. I had walked here earlier by daylight along an old cliff road above the sea that joined the two villages but found now too precipitous to attempt back in this darkness. So I had to wait for a midnight bus, and walked about here for these hours to fill the time. The night wind had come up and gave this place that was still new to me an ominous air and I looked for someone who might look like me.

The festival was centered in a clearing under a loose

improvised webbing of bare light bulbs that began to swing around crazily in the night wind, under which the old man continued to dance in the midst of great mounds of cooking meat tended by beefy men in soiled aprons shouting about in the heat and smoke with the energy of battle, an unbridled energy that contrasted with the old man's spare and subtle moves, who seemed now the fragile poet in the midst of the boisterous warriors whose story he told in mime, the philosopher king interpreting reality's light and shadow show.

Strangely secular by contrast, small groups of priests milled about together in and around the crowds wearing severe black frocks and joyless beards as if to remind the celebrants of their basic Christian design but appearing more earthly than spiritual in this primitive place, like carnival magicians blessing the food and goings-on, well-accepted and fully a part of things. Their leader was familiar. I had been directed to him a few days earlier in a mountain village on the other side of the island to ask permission about taking photographs of religious wall paintings in an ancient little church there. Initially denied by the local priest, the decision had been authoritatively rescinded by this man after a soft ritual questioning about who I was, my family name, grandparents, great-grandparents, villages of their birth, and was I Christian. The decisive fact was that my great-grandfather had been a priest in the nearby mountain village of Kosikia a century earlier, and this man, majestic, tall with flowing white hair and a staff, and clearly crafted by nature to give and deny permissions, knew of him. I felt that I should have asked for more.

Therma sits atop radium hot springs from which it gets its name. Famous for affording miraculous cures for arthritis and other ills, it draws people here from all over the world, singly and in health tours. The springs at Therma have been described as the most radioactive in Europe, indeed, so much so, that certain of them have been closed off in recent years. The remaining springs attract small armies of wide-hipped, hobbled old women in black from this and other islands and lederhosened Europeans who come with their health leaders. The springs are caught and held in dirty little stone buildings scattered crookedly along the shore, about four or five of them, stained and awful like abandoned latrines, smelling of body salts, urine, and the iodine of the sea, each with its own belchings of hot water and steam from deep within the earth, held in great stone tubs like cauldrons where bodies are dipped and sins cooked away, where the suffering immerse themselves in silence contemplating their ills, they come like pilgrims to a healing place but of a religion wholly pagan, without a personified healing force. There is no Christ or Muhammad here, no delegated caring miracler, but only the earth, infinitely more abstract, primitive, and unknowable, the inanimate mother who gives and sustains life, mute and unfeeling, the source of all things. I recalled my childhood image of hell as a steam-filled room with crypt-like tubs holding the bodies of the damned.

The pilgrims in Therma hoped for the earth to heal and not take them, to allow them to sit in its bowel's yield and not be pulled within, here at the periphery of this awesome force from hell caged by a thin canopy of sand and rocks. When they talked they told tales of others who were cured her, like my father who would tell of his father who had been brought here to the springs over the mountains from their village of Kosikia draped like a sack of flour over a mule because he could no longer walk, and who became cured in a week and for forever and went back home on foot.

I recalled the noisy Ikarian *panegeria* of my childhood, depression-era mid-summer picnics held in cow pastures just outside Cleveland or Youngstown or other steel cities of the Great Lakes where my relatives and other Ikarians celebrated the old country way one day each year. As a child I found them bewildering in their intensity. I still recall vividly the appearance of the musicians, three or four old men playing their hearts out for hours sitting on little hard-backed chairs, wearing faces that showed no feeling and smelling of cigars and perspiration. My mother had said they were like that because their wives and children were still in Greece and that they would be better cared for when they could bring them over. As I recall them now, they were like gristled monks working out a penance. For many the time ran out, like old Papayianni who burst into tears one Christmas Day when my brother as a child gave him a Christmas card scrawled in his laborious child's hand, telling Papayianni that he loved him. The old man remembered how he missed his family and that his own children in Ikaria had passed through their childhood without him. I watched him push his thumbs around his eyes to hide his tears from my brother who could not understand why his card would make Papayianni cry.

But it was also difficult for others like my parents who had brought their families over or had married here, and inevitably, to Ikarians. For they had lost the broader interweavings that gave their lives meaning and couldn't really regain it with the few threads they could put together here.

They wept first for what they had left behind, then for what they could not return to, because what they had left had also changed and no longer included them.

For as long as I could remember I was surrounded by an atmosphere of mourning over that loss. We all grieved for it, like an Eden to which none of us could return. Our ancestors had sinned and we had fallen from grace with them, condemned like them to a chronic sense of displacement and separation.

We had lost our way back to the past and were doomed to live in a tawdry present made tolerable only by the customs and artifacts salvaged from that earlier life, surrounded by beings who had no culture of their own, whom we saw as predatory and vulgar, modern-day incarnations of the dreaded barbarians who had plundered and near annihilated our stock by murder, rape, and genetic dilution, and there was great concern in our elders that no further degradation occur here through acculturation. The greatest danger was to the new ones born here like myself, who would have most contact with and temptation by strangers and be least fortified by a strong conviction of the island's ways,since we had never known them directly. We were here with the interface with the *Xeno*, the stranger, *o alathotos*, the unoiled one, carrying in this phrase an echo of the non-Christian, unbaptized invaders of the island—who would tempt us into ill-advised unions with them to generate indistinct intermediary forms no longer pure Ikarian or even pure Greek, spawning hordes of rootless floating progeny, pathetic androids without cultural identity, doomed to nominal bondings with unfaithful spouses, mongrelized in both blood and culture like half-breed Indians doing tribal dances at shopping malls, we would degrade to ruin. Worse than that, we would be ultimately assimilated without a trace, as if eaten to become part of other beings more fit to live in this inhospitable place.

Ironically there was also an abiding sense of shame which some of the older immigrants felt in being identifiable as Greek by non-Greeks, as if the goal was not only to maintain a special identity but to maintain it in secret, as if the outsider who had recognized you as Greek had noticed something that unflatteringly separated you out from others, as if our ways were so subtle that they could be recognized only by us. I think the shame came from their knowledge that they had abandoned something of value, that they had made a mistake, like a mother who puts her child up for adoption and cannot make it make sense to anyone else, as they were asked why they had come and found the answer difficult.

A few of us who were born here stood at the edge of the stream and watched our shapes melt into it. But many did not. Like my brother, they adopted and then enshrined the ways of our parents and kept them and themselves separate and safe and dry like our parents' bodies in their caskets.

Conversations in Ikaria

W e had been staying at the Cabos Hotel on the northern shore of the island of Ikaria and were waiting now for George Longos to wake up. He was supposed to take us this morning to the village of Agios Kirikos on the other side of the island. My cousin Koula, whom I had never met, was holding her best room for us at the Maria Elena Hotel, and we were supposed to be there by noon to take it. And here it was 9:30 already with George still asleep in the lobby and looking terrible.

The manager of the Cabos let George sleep there when he brought in guests arriving on the early morning ferry from Piraeus. Especially if he had other guests like us who would need a cab later the same morning. We were supposed to meet George here in the lobby ready to leave at 9AM but instead found him sleeping face up on the couch with crushed newspapers under his arms and chin like a balled-up feeding bib, not looking like he'd be driving anywhere for a while, least of all the difficult mountain roads between here and Agios Kirikos. A pity to wake him, but we had to get going so I tapped him on the shoulder. He shuddered, stirred slightly, stopped breathing as if to better hear what we would say next, opened his eyes briefly, closed them to rub them with the insides of his wrists, and finally looked up at us to say, yes he was ready, too. He looked terrible.

George had been the only cab driver we had used since we came to this Greek island a week ago even though he was unreliable and pointedly unkempt, needing sleep and a shave at all times. We used him because he knew all my relatives on the island and where they could be found, including my cousin Koula at the Maria Elena Hotel in Agios Kirikos, where we would be staying.

Unfortunately, we also got to know where many of George's relatives could also be found, and that was in the cab as he packed them along with us as free ride-alongs whenever he saw them on the side of the road.

George and his ancient Mercedes were known to everyone on the island and that made it take forever to get anywhere, for besides picking up his relatives, he was stopping to acknowledge everything and everyone, birth sites, accident sites, friends, old customers, passersby, bakery vendors, street sweepers, all without particular point or purpose except perhaps to show us that he was a busy man.

Within a few minutes after leaving the Cabos Hotel, George was soon wrestling his Mercedes along the narrow switchback roads that laced the central ridge of the island on the

the way to Agios Kirikos, which was on the opposite shore of the Cabos. Though there were no people on the mountain roads for George to greet, he would nonetheless stop here and there at a precipice to point out the incipient dangers that his driving skills protected us from. Whenever I would ask rhetorically if many who had not had the benefit of his cab services had gone over at this or that cliff, he would invariably answer in a gesture I knew from my father. It consisted of his tilting his head back slightly with his eyes closed and lips pressed together, and turning his palm downward. The gesture was soft and minimal, the whole of it lasting a second or two, yet wholly unambiguous. His head tilting back slightly signified a negative outcome, his eyes closing that it was irreversible, his lips pressed together that it was unspeakable, and the downward palm that life had become still there. The gesture also carried a second communication, the somewhat paradoxical one that what it signified was not really true, that it was an exaggeration, not to be wholly believed, if at all and, moreover, that I was expected not to. I could see his eyes in the rear-view mirror examining mine to see if I got it. I think that that was what I liked most about George and why we used his cab exclusively.

We were grateful eventually to see the southern shore below and two small villages: one was Chrisostomos, which George identified as the village where my father's mother was born, and just beyond it, the village of Agios Kirikos, our destination this day, and went down the steep curved roads to enter it on its west end. While Agios Kirikos is one of two main harbors of Ikaria, it is only a short walk from one end to the other and only a few minutes by car. harbors of Ikaria, it is only a short walk from one end to the other and only a few minutes by car. We drove past a string of seafront *cafenia* to the east end and onto an oleander-lined street that ended at the Maria Elena Hotel. A three-story white stucco building overlooking the Mediterranean, it was built, owned, and operated by my cousin Koula, whom I had heard of only a few days before and, until now, knew only as a voice on the telephone.

As we pulled up to the hotel a woman suddenly emerged from a side door and into the street before us, apparently surprised to see us right there at that moment. I thought it was a hotel guest but as she jumped out George said it was my cousin Koula. I had never seen her before and was struck by how beautiful she was and by her eyes, which were green, unusual among Greek women and wholly unknown in my family where beauty in women Koula's age ran dark and matronly. She wore a light summer dress that clung unevenly to her body as if pulled on while she was still wet, which I think was probably true since she was in the process of rubbing her hair dry with a large bath towel as she approached us. She walked with her head tilted sideways so that her hair could fall freely and aerate, and while still rubbing it, she circled the cab quizzically, as if trying to see who we were through its dirty windows. (As we found out later, she had just returned from an afternoon swim in the ocean, part of her daily routine, and because we had started so late, as it was already one o'clock, she had no longer expected us today.) George stuck his head out of his window and shouted to her that her cousin from America was here with his wife and what the hell was she doing drying her hair instead of greeting us. She did not reply but continued to circle the cab, peering in one window and then another, and then, as she got around again to the front of the cab, apparently preparing to greet us, George gunned the motor to make his cab lurch forward, forcing Koula to scramble back a few steps against a stone wall, dropping her towel in the process and flailing her arms about as if trapped there, whereupon George jumped out and tried to kiss her and perhaps did. Pushing him away, she turned to us to introduce herself, as if George's antics with her were so common that they wouldn't get in the way of our proper introductions. I got out of the cab and walked over to her, introducing myself and my wife, shook her hand and then, following the custom on the island of greeting female relatives with a kiss on the cheek, I leaned forward, kissed her cheek, and as I did so she whispered in Greek, "I am your cousin," which seemed as if it should have preceded rather than followed the kiss and have been spoken rather than whispered. Moreover, the emphasis was, oddly, not on the Greek word for cousin, which would have been the expected identifier, but rather on the Greek expression for "I am," which made her words take on the different meaning of "I am, after all, your cousin!" suggesting thereby that whatever liberties I had witnessed George take with her, all kissing from me at least would continue to be confined to the cheek area.

I had first heard of Agios Kirikos years ago as the village where my father was to receive mail during his last trip to the island and had chosen to stay, because many of his relatives in Greece either lived in that village or within walking distance of it. There was one particular cluster of my father's nieces and nephews, now in late middle age, who lived just up the hill from the Maria Elena Hotel. Their father had co-owned a restaurant with my father in Cleveland and had dissolved the partnership after an argument with my father and had died shortly afterward, a consequence from which I don't think my father ever recovered.

These were Argyro and her three brothers, Mitchell, Simos, and Nicholas. All but Simos, who had lost a leg from a bullet wound in the turbulent political era here of the early fifties, had lived and worked for some years in America and had returned now to the island to live on their social security. As if a sign that he had been to America, Mitchell insisted on being addressed as "Mitchell" rather than by his Greek name Michali. Their homes were all adjacent to each other on a hillside from which you could see the ocean, and even Turkey on a clear day, built around the original house of their father, which was now occupied by Simos, and on the land their father had owned and which they had inherited from him.

I had wanted in particular to see them, and when we ran across Argyro in Agios Kirikos, she excitedly invited us to come to Simos's house the following evening where she would prepare dinner for all of us.

Argyro had prepared typical Greek food for us and it was the first home-cooked meal we had had in two weeks. There was beef and lamb and pasta and boiled beans, all served lukewarm in the manner of Greek cooking. We were all jammed into Simos's tiny dining room around a table crowded with food, plates, glasses, pitchers, and all of us—Mitchell, Simos, Nicholas and his wife Stella, Argyro, and my wife and myself.

The room seemed ancient with pictures of dead relatives all about, and the dining room opened on one end into the small bedroom where my father had actually stayed in 1955, which completed the sense of a past coming in on us. We talked of what we shared, broadly of family and more narrowly about the food we were eating, for not only was it Greek but it was of the island and, more than that, it was my father's or somebody else's father's favorite food.

Mitchell spoke of his failed marriages with a candor that was unusual among the Greeks I knew in America. The first was to a Polish woman in America and the second to a Greek woman in America and neither worked out, which Mitchell seemed pleased to have survived and to have lived long enough to look back at now as distant. Stella, Nicholas's wife, talked to my wife, who knew no Greek, speaking to her in broken English, alternately holding and releasing my wife's hand in the style of Greek women who like to talk to other women when in the company of men.

After dinner we went out into Simos's patio which was cooler and which he had built himself, as he proudly told us, and we talked more broadly now beyond family and food to the politics of Ayios Kirikos, of the island Ikaria, of Greece, and, ultimately, of America and how much better their life was here on the island.

The talk, while animated, was respectful, pleasant, and subdued and carried on under a breeze that had come up from the sea, and made yet more pleasant by coffee, apricots, and sweets.

Whatever the subject, the talk was purely ritualistic, produced as much for us to jointly hear and enjoy our communal sounds and rhythms as to communicate anything in particular.

Simos's hillside patio was a natural gathering place for neighbors and for people walking after dinner to and from Agios Kirikos below. It was a custom I recalled from my childhood in Cleveland where people were the main recreation and they would all visit each other's houses in the evening. No phone calls or prearrangements. If people visited when you were eating, they would eat with you. If they visited when you were about to go somewhere, they would go there with you. If they visited when you were scolding your children, they would scold them too along with you. And so it was that many passed by Simos's patio that evening and had coffee and conversation with us.

One of the later visitors that evening was a thin bespectacled man named Haralamby, or Harry in English. He was a contractor on the island and had done work for Argyro and her brothers in the past. He had some strong opinions on what was wrong with the island politics as they affected the building trade and seemed to feel generally that he was forced to deal with fools incapable of properly inspecting and passing on his work. He carried with him a somewhat sharper edge than the others and appeared as someone who had something to prove, with a quickness to reply and other ways of gearing his listening to that need. Physically, he was small and unprepossessing, indeed, rather markedly so, something in the manner of the character Woody Allen plays on screen, obscure behind glasses and thinning hair, looking like someone who had just missed a bus or lost an umbrella, but as he talked it became clear that he intended to become dominant among us.

He told a number of extraordinary stories about people he had been forced to deal with in his business, which were increasingly comical. We began to laugh a great deal more than we had before he came, and in order to account for our hilarity I had now to translate his stories to my wife who did not understand Greek and since what he was saying had no context save that which his stories brought with him, she felt she needed to know more exactly what he was saying. She had earlier been pleased to witness the cadence of our interactions without needing to know exactly what anyone was saying. But that was before Harry joined us.

Harry was now entering into an increasingly hilarious mood and into the main story that was to feed it. It was a story about a sexual misadventure of his with a very heavy and aggressive woman. He had swept into the story very suddenly and I missed its beginnings and didn't really know if the others knew the woman he was talking about or, indeed, if she was entirely fictional, but it really did not matter.

The story quickly became more comical as Harry contrasted the woman's strength and massiveness with his own weakness and thinness, which he had by now convincingly projected to us so that he seemed at times incapable of continuing, almost as if eroding in the telling, and to the point where the recounting of the narrative itself appeared in jeopardy. All other conversation had ceased and Stella had stopped bringing in coffee and apricots and sat down with us to listen to Harry, mesmerized as much by the growing weakness in his voice as by the content of his story. As he got weaker the story became more remarkable and bizarre, as if he were dissolving to become fuel for it. Moreover, he had subtly given the story an allegorical spin wherein he and the woman were now characters in a Greek myth, in which she became the voluptuous seductress and he the reluctant serpent. With that he began to writhe, standing up to do so, twisting and turning his torso and pulling his arms over himself to illustrate the agony of his attempts to escape her as she crushed him under her weight and held him fast between her massive thighs, and ultimately to consummation. He began to perspire heavily as he told the story and his breathing became uneven and labored as his writhing intensified and he flailed his arms in frantic swimming motions in the air to show how he was trying to escape. As he could not meet her physical demands and was unable to escape, he began to beg her to release him, and screamed aloud in an anguished falsetto as if to the woman in the story to release him, as he saw that he could not move her to pity nor induce us, his audience, to intercede, and that she was intent to have her way with him. In the telling the serpent metamorphosed to became Harry's penis, which drove the story to a greater complexity and artfulness, where Harry's writhings and twistings were taken then with these new meanings, so that his movements had now to be reinterpreted in a more pornographic vein. And suddenly Harry ended his story by bursting into laughter to become released from its telling, leaving us to complete this triple overlay of images as we would.

Harry had told the story well and artfully but in the telling had sucked all the energy in the patio into his own small space, leaving us with little to say to him or to each other, as we groped about a bit for where we were before he had come to join us. But the rhythm of our talking to each other was gone now, and there was no bringing Harry into it, so we looked to Harry to tell us more, that being all that seemed left to do. But as if he had already gone further than he had intended to, and sensing his resulting isolation, he got up, thanked us, and left.

Kosikia

M y parents came to America from the island of Ikaria in the Aegean sea thirty kilometers off the coast of Turkey which had once cast a shadow on the island of which the islanders still speak and who retained a wariness of anyone who speaks a language other than Greek. They had each come from a mountain village on the island whose rocky slopes and harsh winter winds had conditioned villagers to endure by virtue of their being so like one another and in the communal memory of struggles against the *Varvari*—the Turkish barbarians from the east—who had once sought to dilute their bloodline, their talk of them now more ritualistic than real, belonging to the distant past yet strong enough to serve bonds that held them now together even though those enemies that had once so threatened them ceased to be.

I went to visit Ikaria with my wife who was not Greek, to visit the mountain villages from which they had come, a journey motivated more out of curiosity than expectation, and found these villages exhilaratingly real, so different from the sheltered enclave my family had built around themselves in America, yet so similar.

My parents' villages were both situated in the mountainous central spine of the island and I found them more than simply rustic: they were primitive, beyond anything that I had expected, seemingly unchanged over generations, even centuries. My mother's village of Arethusa and my father's village of Kosikia were each little more than a steep hillside sprinkling of tiny houses hewn out of gray rock, plaster, and slate amid clusterings of olive trees. The villagers themselves appeared to live without benefit of outside help or authority to summon one if needed, where the sick or injured would heal of themselves or die, according as divine will chose it to be, a will consulted daily in a near-pagan version of Christian beliefs wherein God's workings were seen by villagers as actively directing not only their personal fortunes but the movement of every natural and supernatural process around them, to include the activities of angels and lesser deities intermingling with ghosts of the dead in intermittent yet common visitations, all of which, ironically, served to soften the otherwise spare and unforgiving harshness of life around them.

Our journey this day was to my father's village of Kosikia, distinguished by being surrounded by near-vertical sheets of rock almost a thousand feet high, which only wild mountain goats could traverse. Moving about in the village had to be done on foot or by mule and could be done safely only in daylight Though the road leading up to the village could be driven by auto, there were only rocky footpaths connecting the road to the houses there.

The house in which my father had lived was still intact and habitable, indeed occupied by two aged cousins of his with whom my father had shared his childhood and to whom his father, my grandfather, upon leaving the island, gave them the right to live there in perpetuity.

We had been driven to Kosikia by George Longos, the cab driver we had been using to drive us along the coastal villages of the island from the seaside hotel in which we had been staying. George had been used to driving my father and uncles when they had traveled to the island in more recent years and we had inherited him as part of a family tradition to use him when visiting here. Not to say that there were not advantages in using him, for he was very familiar with every road and village on the island and, more importantly, knew where all my relatives here lived and where those who had died were buried, the location of every patch of ground that our family ever owned, and to such a level of detail that I wondered if he might even be related to us somehow. I ventured once to ask him if this was so and he answered me in the way my father did, by tilting his head back slightly and half closing his eyes, to dismiss a question of mine as unworthy of being responded to, a gesture so like my father's as to keep the question alive for me.

George also seemed very knowledgeable about physical and historical aspects of the island, its geography, its earthquake faults, its history of Turkish, then Italian, then German occupation, the last two occupations which he triumphantly announced he had lived through, and generally, it seemed, knowledgeable about everything. George never let on that he could not answer something, it being a point of pride with him to be regarded as extremely knowledgeable. Some of his inclination to appear learned may have been stimulated by my once having remarked to him that I had been a schoolteacher in America, which suddenly seemed to heighten his interest to show me what he knew.

He had been driving a cab here for at least twenty-five years, dating at from when my father had made his first return visit to the island from America, and perhaps in the old Mercedes he still used. Besides, George himself seemed to have relatives everywhere, indeed, even here in Kosikia, where he told us that a great uncle related to his wife's father had some goats and a vineyard up here, and that one of his goats had butted the old man and knocked him to the ground so that he couldn't work as well as before, and appreciated George's visiting him once in a while to bring him a bottle of Masticha, a favorite liquor on the island and much favored by the old man.

My wife, who had patiently endured my talking to George in Greek, not a word of which she understood, seemed less impressed with him and often suggested, whenever I told her something George had recounted, that he may have made the whole thing up, just to impress me. Nonetheless, she regarded him as good-willed, as did I, and allowed that he was perhaps embellishing his explanations to better entertain us, as when he had told us that the name Kosikia came from the word *kosifikia*, which meant, according to George, situated at a very high altitude, and my wife had looked up the word in a Greek dictionary she carried around in her bag and found that that word didn't even appear in it.

George had parked his Mercedes at the point where the road ended, got out with us and proceeded to accompany us on foot along some precipitous trails and up to a tiny house, which he pointed out as the one that my grandfather had owned and in which my father himself had lived. With an air of seeming confidentiality, he warned us that the only occupants of the house now were two aged sisters, cousins of my father's, one well into her nineties and the other at least one hundred years of age. Neither had ever married for reasons, George said, he didn't want to go into. Since he seemed to show little reticence to gossip about everyone, I assumed that he simply had no knowledge about this. He motioned us to follow him as he walked up to an open door in front of the house, then without knocking proceeded to shout that my father's eldest son and his wife were here to visit and where the hell was everybody. He turned back to us with a wry smile and said that because these old women couldn't hear well, shouting our presence was the best way to get their attention.

And it did, as an old woman with a large black mole on her chin who looked as if out of a child's fairy tale came to the door to greet us. She stared at us for a moment as the driver repeated in a loud voice who we were and that we were visiting from America.

I wondered if she could understand what our driver was saying but realized that she was only studying our faces and taking her time in doing so. I had already accepted as the custom on the island that in being introduced to villagers, they would invariably try to match your face against those of others whom they knew, in tracking ancestry, an important connection here. The old woman spent little time on my wife's face, which she recognized immediately as non-Greek and stared at me for a full minute before speaking.

There were tears in her eyes as she appeared to recognize my father's face in mine and reached her bony hand to grasp mine.

"This is Kiria Agnostopoulou," George said to me in the way of introductions, smiling as if forcing a formality unaccustomed for both the old woman and for him and, while proper, I felt it mockingly done for our benefit. He had used the genitive form for her last name which was customary in formal speech in Greek in addressing an unmarried woman, as it signified that she was still in possession of her father, even one, as in this case, who had long been dead. It was clear that she had never before heard George address her that way, as he added with a smile, "You can call her by her first name, Kalliope," he said, drawing then a smile from the old woman's face, as he expected, as he next introduced me and my wife to her.

The old woman beckoned us into her tiny living room, and motioned us to sit at a table at its center on which a pink ceramic bowl was placed with a cloth napkin over it. She waved her hand toward a second old woman, who was sitting on a couch on the side of the room combing out her hair, which was long and gray and apparently a point of pride with her. She appeared not to have yet noticed us or at least gave no sign that she did, as her gaze was directed to the open doorway through which we had entered. George winked at us as if to acknowledge that this second woman was fully aware of our presence and only pretending not to be, for she was waiting to be introduced. George turned to her, walked up to her in an exaggeratedly deferential manner, took her hand in his, held it, and looked back at us. Then, using the same overly formal introduction he had just used with her sister, only now with an increased air of solemnity, announced loudly in Greek for her benefit, "This is Kiria Agnostopoulou." He then added, in broken English, "But you can call her by her first name, Eirini." Turning to the old woman, he repeated, "Eirini," and asked her in Greek if his and our using her first name was acceptable to her, again with seemingly mocking formality The old woman nodded to us as if acknowledging it was acceptable to her, all the while continuing to comb her hair. George turned to us and explained in broken English, that Eirini was over one hundred years old and could no longer hear well enough to converse fluidly, and was combing her hair as we saw because she wanted to look her best.

I was struck not only by the small size of the room and the odd ways of these two old women, but also by a number of old sepia-colored photographs that provided the décor of the room. There were several dozen of them pinned or pasted up along one wall and I recognized them all as photographs of my family that were similar to other photographs I had seen in my parents' photo albums and which I understood to have been taken shortly before they left for America. Kalliopi walked up to the wall and pointed to the largest of the photographs: it was of my grandparents and all seven of their children, my father among them as a young man of nineteen. She explained that this was a photograph that had been taken on the very day they had all left the island for America, a day that she said she would never forget. I looked over at the other old woman on the couch to tell her how I imagined that had been a very sad day for her as well and saw, as she continued to comb her hair, that she was weeping. Then my attention turned to Kalliope, who had come up to the table at which we were sitting and removed the napkin that had been covering the ceramic plate at the center to exhibit a pile of more photographs of the family.

George Longos, who had been silent as this unveiling was taking place, finally said to me in Greek, "These photographs have been on that wall and in this old plate on the table ever since I can remember. These old women kept them just so, which is their way of keeping daily connection with your father's family. They are your father's cousins; their father and your grandfather were brothers. There is no one else alive who is more closely related to them. These photographs are their only link."

At this point the two women were not saying anything. They continued to stare at my wife and me as if we, too, were ghosts. The mood here began to feel very dark to me, and I had a sudden impulse to get out, to get back to our hotel.

George had moved to stand in the open doorway, as if to indicate that he was ready to leave if we were. I looked away from both women for fear that looking at them in what I regarded as their awful vulnerability in living this way with a long-dead past would embarrass them, and I turned my attention to George. He shrugged his shoulders and looked at my wife and me, apparently waiting for some signal from me about what I wanted to do. The seated old woman, Eirini, suddenly raised her hand and beckoned Kalliopi to come to her. The three of us watched as Eirini drew Kalliopi's ear to her lips and whispered something. Kalliopi stood up smartly and announced in Greek that she had not been properly attending to her visitors from America and that we were not to leave until she had gotten some refreshments out for us.

Kalliopi helped Eirini to the table and brought out a bottle of Masticha ouzo and some cookies on a plate. George explained to me in Greek in a loud voice so the two sisters could appreciate what he was saying, that the resin on which Masticha ouzo is based and out of which the cookies were made is obtained from plants on the southern coast of the island of Chios, fifty-six miles north of Ikaria, and is exported throughout the world for both confectionery and distillery purposes. George gave me a long look after this description, as if to see me acknowledge the breadth of his knowledge.

After we had had a few glasses of ouzo and were feeling its effects, the two sisters distributed the photographs on the table before us and haltingly recounted that terrible day when the family had left. While I was wholly taken with the feelings these two old creatures showed as they drew their bony hands over something so distant in the past and yet so alive for them, I was aware that George seemed less moved than I as he leaned over to me to suggest that, if it was all right with my wife and me, he would like to visit his great-uncle while he was up here and to give him a bottle of Masticha ouzo he had brought up for him. He added that, if we wanted to stay here visiting with the sisters, he could come back for us or, if we liked, we would be more than welcome at his great-uncle's house but that, in any case, it would not be safe to attempt it after dark, adding somberly, that a tourist from America who did not even have any relatives here had stumbled in the dark off a mountain path near George's great-uncle's house the year before and had fallen to his death. George pressed his lips together and raised his eyebrows to ensure that he'd made his point on this. It was clear that George wanted to leave and that he preferred not to have to come back for us.

Peter G. Tripodes

Plagia

More an isolated and forgotten place than a village, Plagia lies on the desolate southern coast of the island of Ikaria, where a few shepherds with no fortune elsewhere herd their goats along the cliffs high above the Aegean Sea. Old Stavro, a cousin of my grandfather, was one of them, and my wife and I were to visit him that day.

Our driver, George Longos, whom I had preferred not to use again if at all possible, was waiting for us in the lobby of the Maria Elena hotel in Ayios Kirikos, a harbor town about fifty kilometers from Plagia, ready to take us there in his old Mercedes, and wouldn't hear of our using anyone else and, as ever, ready to make a day of it with us, which made it expensive, especially as he preferred to calculate costs in his head, insisting it was cheaper without a meter because he would round off costs in our favor and that was, he said, out of respect for my father, who had visited here years earlier.

The Maria Elena was owned and operated by my cousin Koula with whom George had a running flirtation and so didn't mind waiting around all day for us or anyone else who might need a cab when he had nothing else to do.

The road to Plagia was unpaved, twisted, and deeply fissured, edged between a mountain and a cliff opening below over what must have been a thousand feet to the sea. As usual, George drove with an air of confidence through the island roads, though this one taxed him more than usual as he bravadoed through its turns, adding that very few drivers would have ventured it, that we were lucky to have him, that transportation was typically by mule, and that even that was dangerous, and that it was not unusual for an occasional mule to slip and fall into the sea. Maybe two a year he said, shaking his head in mock sadness and holding up two fingers to underscore it.

"Goats too," he added solemnly after a moment's silence. "Sure-footed as they are, they fall off these cliffs too." I saw him looking back at us in his rear-view mirror to see if we were fully listening. "Yes," he said more loudly in case we weren't, "Old Stavro lost a goat over the cliff while he was tending a bunch of them, a sure-footed beast it was, like the others, but not careful enough it seems," then shook his head and whistled through his teeth to make this point as well, and adding, "Very dangerous up here, you've got to be careful," as he stuck his head out the window, apparently to look down the cliff at the sea. "The water's pretty rough down there today." He laughed as he added, "I sure wouldn't want to fall from here." Abruptly, he turned the wheel rapidly left and right as if to avoid something in the road, but apparently did it to make the Mercedes lurch and alarm us. I watched him smile in the rear-view mirror as he ran his index finger across his throat. "But don't worry about me, though. You don't have to. Because I know this road so well I could drive it in my sleep." As he said that, he laughed again and, for my benefit, as he closed his eyes for a moment as if feigning sleep.

"How far is it to Stavros's?" I asked in English so that my wife, who wasn't Greek, could follow what we were saying and George's answer was as I expected, both flip and in Greek, "*Oso makria eine*," its meaning being, as far as it is, which sounded less nonsensical in Greek, but not much.

"What did he say?" my wife asked. He said, "As far as it is."

"Great," she said, unimpressed. "We shouldn't have come out here on a road like this."

"There's no other road to Stavros's," I said, feeling, however, the same as she.

George leaned his head back as if in an effort to get into the conversation and, as he did so, the cab lurched to the right and into the side of the mountain, its fender brushing against a rock. "No need to fear, missus," he said in broken English, "I know this road the way I know my own palm," which he kissed and held up his hand, turning his palm toward us.

"Don't you worry," he said, "this old Mercedes will get us there. It knows the way," he added, smiling back at us in his mirror.

"How old is Stavro?" I asked.

"Old," he said, "I don't know how he still gets around those rocks. It's like the Devil put them there to torture him. Old Stavro can hardly move to track his goats around them."

George's mood seemed to have darkened somewhat, maybe from scraping his fender. I wondered if he'd charge me for that, add something to the cab fare to cover it. I had no way of telling because every time I got George to take me somewhere, he'd just act like he was calculating in his head and come up with a number, as if I shouldn't question it because he kept it low because of my father for whom he had had a lot of respect, and that I was fortunate to have a father like that, someone who commanded respect.

George suddenly let out an exclamation and stopped the car. He stuck his head out the window up to his shoulders, drew himself back in again and wiped his forehead with an old rag he had on his dashboard. "No problem," he said. "My front wheel on the left is off the road."

"Off the road?"

"Yes," he said, "Off the road. The wheel is just sticking out there."

"Should we get out of the car?"

"No, just you and your wife sit way over on the other side to balance the car while I back up," which he did, then sat up, looked back at us and laughed. "Don't you worry. I know these roads like I know the palm of my hand," which he held up again to show us.

"Don't you or your wife worry," he said, as we started up again. "I'll get you there all right," he added, making the sign of the cross. "Do you know how many cars have gone off the road back there?"

"How many?"

"Plenty," George said, "plenty," as he added, "You two can relax now. There it is, old Stavro's place."

"Where?" I asked, seeing nothing.

"There," George said, pointing to a tiny hut at the end of a path several hundred feet from the road. "They live there. Stavro and his wife. He built it himself. They live there winter and summer. Can you believe it? They'll be happy to see you."

"Why?"

"Because they would be happy to see anyone. Out here no one is expecting anyone but are happy with anyone. Stavro is your cousin? Right? His door is always open to his cousins."

"No. He's my grandfather's cousin."

"Same thing," George said as he leaned on his horn. "I'm letting him know he's got relatives come to visit him."

"Maybe no one is here," I said.

"Only if they're dead they're not here," he said, "no one here goes anywhere."

George suddenly shouted, "There he is, old Stavro, see him?" I looked and saw someone who appeared to be very tiny and aged, maybe close to a hundred, as they get to be around here I've heard. He was edging his way out the door of his hut and onto the path. He stared our way for an instant, and then motioned us to come toward him. I turned to George, "Thanks. Are you coming in, too?"

"No," he said. "I'll just wait in the cab," making a sign for me to take my time visiting my relative, the more time the better. It was George's way.

My wife and I walked up the path and approached Stavro. He stood no more than five feet tall and looked more weathered than anyone I'd ever seen, and I wondered what he did here, what he could do here. As we reached him, he got up on his toes and kissed my cheek, in the custom of old-world Greeks, mentioning my grandfather's name, then leaning back and staring at me as if studying my face to see if he could see my grandfather in it, and when he couldn't, he shook his head and began to cry, as if my grandfather remained irretrievable to him. He asked me my name as if verifying that I was really who I was supposed to be, and motioned toward my wife with a tilt of his head as if to ask, "Who is she?" for it was clear to him that she wasn't Greek and so even less likely for him to find anyone looking like her that he knew.

I told him I was sorry to hear about his goat, and he looked at me looked at me quizzically. The one that had fallen off the cliff and into the sea, I explained. The old man smiled, and then told me that that had never happened. I looked back at George standing next to his cab and saw him laughing, that even from a couple hundred feet old Stavro had figured that George had played a joke on me. Stavro then waved his hand across his chest to show that it was no matter, none at all, and whistled low like a ground bird to summon a very tiny woman who slowly emerged from the hut, unbelievably smaller than Stavro and appearing even older, and coming out to stand with him. "*E kyria mou*," Stavro said, using a respectful version of "my missus" in Greek, though in the manner of country people at the time, he never said her name, only her relationship to him. She nodded toward my wife and me without speaking, looked past us at George standing next to his cab and nodded also to him. She then turned and walked towards the hut, beckoning us with a gesture to follow her in.

The entry door was low, scarcely over Stavro's head, so low that my wife and I had to bend over sharply to enter, which we did, then to find ourselves standing in a small windowless room, dark even in late afternoon sun, and feeling like giants in the shadowy hut of two elves.

Stavro followed us in and motioned for us to sit on what

appeared to be a bed, the only one in the room, pushed against one corner and no more than a homemade mattress stuffed with rags and sitting atop bales of dried grasses, I supposed feed for his goats when needed.

Stavro drew up a stool and placed it next to the makeshift bed, sat down on it without speaking, studied my wife's face for a moment, then turned to me. "*Then eine elinitha,*" he said, whose meaning was, she isn't Greek, then half closed his eyes for an instant as if to say that that wasn't too bad, yet not what he would have preferred. He motioned to his own wife who was standing next to him, curled his hand and brought it up to his mouth and tilted his head back as if drinking, whereupon she made her way to the other corner of the room, opened the door of a small wooden cabinet and brought out a jar containing a clear liquid over what appeared to be a gum-like residue that had settled on the bottom.

She shook the jar till the residue had mixed in with the liquid, clouding it, then brought out a small cup and buffed its lip against her sleeve. "I think that's something for us," I said, turning to my wife.

"Not for me," she said sharply, "Did you see that mold on the bottom that she shook loose?"

"It doesn't matter," I said, "We're their guests here and they would take it as an affront if we refused."

Stavro watched our interchange and motioned to his wife who buffed the lip of the cup again and poured a small amount from the jar into it, then handed the cup to Stavro. My wife leaned over to whisper to me, "I wouldn't drink much of that if were you. You don't want to get sick out here in this remote place where I don't know the language."

"George out there knows enough English to be able to help you," I said, mock-seriously.

Stavro watched and waited patiently until we were through, then walked up and held the cup out to me, holding it in both hands as if a sacrament. I held my hand out as he placed it in my hand with both his hands still around it, which he finally released as he nodded to me, a signal I supposed that I was to drink from it now. I took a sip and found that it tasted like fermented almonds. I smiled and raised the cup to show my approval. He and his wife watched as I took another sip, which surprisingly now tasted stronger than the first and made my tongue smart.

I smiled up at Stavro and his wife, who were standing staring at me as if they expected more of a response. "*Eine kalo,*" I said, meaning, it is good, then added in an effort to be more responsive, "*yevstikos,*" meaning savory, which brought the first smile to his wife's face, and her first words, "*eine mezes,*" which meant that it was a delicacy. This prompted me to take yet another sip after which I nodded appreciatively, feeling increasingly settled in, relaxed for the first time since leaving Ayios Kirikos that morning, and I offered some to my wife who smiled up at our hosts then turned and said softly to me, "We should go."

"Why?"

"Because we can't stay too long here. George is out there with his cab, waiting. Besides, it's a long drive back, and you're not looking quite right to me."

Stavro seemed to understand every word we said, for at that point he walked to the doorway of the hut, stepped out onto the footpath and whistled. In no more than a minute, George appeared, stooping as he entered the small hut, which seemed now full to bursting with George's effusive manner and loud talking as he animatedly exchanged greetings with Stavro and his wife, who seemed themselves now suddenly more animated, abandoning the formality they had earlier shown to my wife and me.

George was talking loudly about how the road up here had gotten worse since he had last been here and how he doubted now that it might even be a problem for him to drive us back and that he was sure no one else would have ever attempted driving here in the first place, and that he would have to hazard the trip back seeing there was no way that Stavro and his wife could put up the three of us here. He sighed with an air of resignation that he had no choice but to drive us back soon and hoped that God would see fit to have us survive the return part of the trip.

When George was finished with his little speech, he slapped Stavro on the back, laughed, then stepped over to Stavro's fragile little wife to hold her in a bear-like hug and whisper loudly to her in Greek, "Oh you beautiful thing, you. When old Stavro dies, you look out because no matter how bad the road is, I'll be coming up here for you!" Stavro and his wife joined George in laughter, with Stavro then telling George how much he had missed him.

George then turned to me and seeing the cup in my hand, asked me, with a wink, what I thought of it. "Very good," I said in English for my wife's benefit. George raised his eyebrows in mock puzzlement, then turned to Stavro and winked again. I began to wonder if this was another joke here being played on me. Yet I enjoyed watching this other aspect of our hosts unfolding with George now in the room and waited to see if they would also offer that special drink to him. When they did not, I supposed at the time that it was a special drink brought out only for special guests and that George was too familiar to them to be treated in a special way, or that there was something peculiar about that drink of which I should have been more wary. I realized only later that they had only that one cup, and that it was already in use by me.

I drained it and handed the empty cup back to her. Stavro reached over and clasped my hand in both of his and shook it vigorously. I bowed slightly to his wife and said in Greek how nice it had been to meet my grandfather's cousin at long last, and said that I hoped to return one day. George rolled his eyes as if marking how unlikely that was ever to happen, then clapped Stavro on the shoulder and kissed his cheek. "*Lipon, fevgome,*" he said to all of us as a group, an announcement meaning, "and so, we leave," and intoned solemnly as if the last scene of a play, George ever mindful of the moment. My wife shook our hosts' hands and absent-mindedly shook George's too, as if she was planning to stay. Stavro's wife laughed, apparently more relaxed now, and we laughed with her. Following a gesture from George we turned to follow him down the path back to his cab. We waved back to our hosts as we approached the cab and got in. George turned the cab around and leaned on the horn in a series of rapid bursts as our hosts waved back at us, and we were on our way back to Ayios Kirikos.

George said it was important to get to Ayios Kirikos before dark because on a moonless night this road becomes undrivable, and began to drive back at what seemed an unsafe speed. He looked back at me I think to see if I thought he was driving too fast, a move which made him take his eyes off the road for an instant and simultaneously to cock the wheel toward the cliff. My wife screamed as George quickly righted the cab just at the edge of a precipice. George laughed and said, in Greek, don't look down. My wife poked me in the ribs as if to prod me to scold George to slow down, which I couldn't. His competence and daring were what he wore for us and I hesitated to say anything that would diminish it.

Not one to allow silence for long, George began to sing a song about how traveling by car on a mountain road was much better than traveling by mule, and he pitched and rocked himself and the cab mimicking the sway of the beast.

He looked back at us in his rear-view mirror and stopped his singing to apologize for scaring us and to tell us that while the tune was from a very old song from his childhood, he had made up new words for it to fit the perils of our journey, and was that all right with us. Without waiting for an answer, he began again to sing, at first loudly, then letting his voice trail off.

I closed my eyes and tried to sleep, yet aware that my wife was still nervously watching the road. She had never liked nor trusted George and had confided to me that she worried that in some mindless gesture of bravado he'd manage to have us all killed.

I felt the cab suddenly stop, looked up, and saw that George had pulled over to the side of the road and thrown his arm over the back of the passenger seat. He was looking directly back at us. "I want you to see this," he said in Greek, "It's the village of Chrisostomos where your father's mother Vasiliki was born, look, please, your family roots are here. Look."

My wife and I looked out the window of the cab down the side of a steep hillside at a row of houses scattered between groves of olive trees and edged to the sea.

"Where?" I asked.

"You're looking too far down," he said, "into the newer part of the town. Your grandmother wasn't born in a house by the sea. It wasn't safe to live near the sea in those days, exposed to the view of pirates who cruised these waters. You have to look up here closer to the road, those houses there, she was born in one of them, in one of these."

I couldn't quite see what George was referring to. All I could see were rocks and vegetation. "Let's go outside," I said to my wife, "where we can get a better look at what he's talking about." George came out from his side of the cab and pointed to what appeared to be an undergrowth of foliage all but covering the ruins of some old stone houses, now abandoned and embedded in the hillside, and crumbling into the earth under their protective canopy.

As we looked down, George rubbed his temples with his thumbs, as if deep in thought. "Yes, I know now, it is that one," he exclaimed, pointing to what appeared to be the remains of a slate roof over a low wall tilted crazily into the earth. That was the roof of Vasiliki's house, which, of course, didn't look like that then.

George appeared to be increasingly given to making identifications like this one, pointing out some property or remains of one, and declaring it to have belonged to an ancient relative of mine and hinting at some current value it might now have to me. My wife had warned me that George might be making much of this up to ingratiate himself to us as a guide to our family history. "He knows that he can say anything to us because we don't know differently."

I really didn't care, though, if what he said was literally

true, as long as something like it might be true. My wife knew that turn of mind in me, and warned that my regarding George's pronouncements as factual only encouraged him to tell more lies. For me that was all right too. "Are you sure, George, that that's the house," I had asked.

"Of course I'm sure," he said, "I know this island and, what's more, I know your family. May their souls be at rest," he added, making the sign of the cross. My wife looked at me and rolled her eyes.

George must have noticed for, as if to bolster his claims, he expanded on how serious the pirate problem had been in my grandmother's time and that, unbeknownst to me in those years well before my father's birth, my grandmother might well have been seized or murdered in the pirates' plundering escapades, and that the history of our ancestors' survival could not be separated from who we were now.

"Can we walk down to those houses, maybe to hers?" I asked, avoiding my wife's glance. George shook us off with a wave of his hand and a grimace, and said to me in Greek that it was too dangerous, which I relayed to my wife. "But there are children running in and around those ruins there," she said, "If they can play in them, it should be safe enough for us." I pointed them out to George and asked again if we could go down and see, whereupon George painstakingly explained that they were not Greek children but children of gypsies, Bulgarian gypsies, scavengers really, they were all over the island and carried diseases so it was best not to get too close to them. I explained that to my wife who snapped back at me that George was making up more lies to suit what he wanted us to believe, and that I should get George to take us directly back to Ayios Kirikos since there was nothing that he would let her see here that interested her. My wife later confided to me that she thought the reason George dissuaded us from looking more closely at the houses was that we would find something there that would expose his story about my grandmother and these houses and her having once lived in one of them was wholly fabricated.

"Let's go then," my wife said, "if there's nothing more to see here, let's get back to Ayios Kirikos."

George knew enough English to understand. For suddenly he burst out in Greek, "Not before we say hello to my cousin who lives in the new part of Chrisostomos below, down there by the beach." I remarked to George that I didn't know he had a cousin here and that he should have told us earlier so that we could have planned that into our day. Besides, he would probably be figuring the time spent here into his billing. Never explicit, for George didn't work that way, he'd just give us a number at the end of the day, always adding that it was a cut-rate price because of the respect he had for my family, and punctuated with a subtle lift of his eyebrows.

Not wanting to press him on it, I still felt I had to ask: "How many cousins do you have here in Ikaria, George?"

"More than I can tell you," he said in Greek, "more than

I can tell you," his voice trailing off as if it was a burden for him to keep track of all his relatives. "But this one is special," he said, suddenly more brightly, "and we certainly can't leave Chrisostomos without looking her up.

"Her?" I asked, "Are all your cousins women?"

"You might say that," George said with a smile. "You might just say that."

I explained to my wife what the conversation with George was about. "His cousin here? Do you believe that?" she asked irritably. "He's probably got a woman here who is no relation to him and he's using us to visit her, to show her he's a big shot with family connections with rich Americans who believe whatever he says."

"Well he does seem to know a lot of people on the island, in Ayios Kirikos and everywhere, you have to give him that."

"How can you tell what he really knows when he's probably lying half the time? You're just allowing yourself to be taken in by him."

George must have understood something of her concern for he asked again, now in a soft more imploring voice, "Please, just a few minutes to see my cousin. She lives just below."

We got back into the cab and George steered it onto a path that led down from the mountain road to the new Chrisostomos village below. This path was much more precipitous and uneven than the main road had been, and strewn with rocks that George blithely drove his cab over, causing terrible intermittent scraping sounds under the old Mercedes, all of which George seemed wholly oblivious to.

The village of new Chrisostomos was very beautiful and though referred to as new, it was very ancient looking. As we approached it from above, we could see an old traditional oil press with its mill building and its millstone still intact, which George explained animals still turned to grind the olives, and that we shouldn't underestimate the importance of this little village inasmuch as the region around it was quite famous as a major center of the island's olive oil production industry and, he added after a pause, "also famous for its beautiful women," as he pinched his fingers together to bring them to his lips.

After a short, winding downhill ride we drove along a white and green ensemble of houses arranged along the shoreline like an amphitheater and stopped when we reached a small house at the end ensconced under a sheltering trellis of grape vines. George stopped the cab, turned off the engine and said his cousin lived here. He motioned us to wait in the cab till he found out if his cousin was at home. We watched him walk up to the front door, open it without knocking, and go in. That was followed in a few seconds by wild screams and laughter as George and a young woman, his arm tightly around her waist, emerged. George brought her up to the cab, his arm still around her, and motioned us to get out to meet her. As we did, George announced, "This is my cousin Koula. She speaks a little English, so you can talk with her," whereupon the young woman added, "a leetle," holding her hand up to show a small space between thumb and index finger.

I remarked that Koula must be a popular name on the island, since my own cousin who owned the Maria Elena hotel in Ayios Kirikos was also named Koula, whereupon the young woman said in heavily accented English that Koula was not her real name but that George called her that and that it was all right with her.

"Yes," George shouted in Greek as he comprehended a bit of what we were saying, and stepped up to her, his face to hers, saying: "Yes, you are, you, my sweet little Koula you will always be to me." He suddenly leaned further into her and tried to kiss her on the lips, but she turned abruptly to face us, saying that we had not yet been introduced.

I was surprised to hear George introduce us as his cousins, adding that perhaps because of that we were also cousins of hers, cousins who had come all the way from America to meet any of our cousins who might be here, right here in Chrisostomos and what good luck it was that Koula was here to be visited, just as he flashed her a wink and made one last attempt to plant a kiss on her lips, at which he failed again.

"What was all that?" my wife asked.

"Just lying a little about his being related to us."

"A little? He's not related to you, is he? I hope not."

"Not as far as I know," I said, suppressing a smile.

"Thank God," she said, which drew a smile from Koula, who understood our interchange. It was also clear to us that we who could no longer speak English with impunity, for Koula understood everything.

It was George's turn now to be puzzled, as he asked her in Greek what her smile was about. She told him, and in feigned distress, he slapped his forehead as if in the belated realization that he had lied to us, and spoke the only words of English that he seemed comfortable with: "No matter," he said in English and then immediately asked Koula in Greek what she had in the house for us to eat.

"What is he saying?" my wife asked, suspiciously.

"He wants her to feed us."

"My God. He's really uncivilized."

"No," I said, "It's the island way to feed anyone who comes to your door, although you usually don't have to ask to be fed. Food is usually offered immediately."

"Well, George did ask, didn't he? That's what I mean by uncivilized."

"It's still within island etiquette," I said.

Koula, who understood this too, tried to assure us: "Don't worry about it, that's George. He's very direct. We're used to him." She waved her hand toward George, who had already taken a seat at the table and was looking about apparently to see what preparations Koula was making to feed him. "Well, where is it?" he asked playfully. "I'm starving."

Koula cautioned him to wait as she opened the door of an old-fashioned wooden icebox and drew out a large tureen of soup.

"*Eine Avgolemono*," she said, and then turned to us adding, "Egg lemon soup."

"*Avgolemono!*" he shrieked, as if overwhelmed at the prospect of having some soon, and raised his arms, shouting "*Thavmasios!*" meaning that it was miraculous that she would have on hand his favorite soup and then in a single sweep of appreciation, he seized Koula's hands and pulled her off balance and onto his lap, where he finally succeeded in planting a loud kiss on her lips, exclaiming in Greek, "and that's for you, my little bird who serves me a wonderful soup." She pulled back, stood up, straightened her skirt, and laughed loudly as she stepped back away from him, perhaps to show us that George's antics in no way unsettled her.

My wife leaned over to me and whispered, "Whatever you think of him, I have to say that I don't like him and his crude ways, not at all. He's a chauvinist of the worst kind. How can you put up with him!"

I also wondered why I didn't find George more offensive than I did. As if reading my thoughts, Koula said, "*Eine phigouratsis, tipotis allo*," meaning that George was a performer and show-off and nothing more and that his ways were fully acceptable in these remote villages here where they enlivened things.

Peter G. Tripodes

Encounters

A Caretaker for Mrs. Kalosoma

C hristina only nineteen yet looking older in the black that she and her mother wore during their mourning.

Mr. Kalosoma came visiting also wearing a black suit to show his respect. "I'm deeply sorry to hear about Mr. Orony's death," he said.

"And we're sorry to hear of your wife's illness," Mrs. Orony replied. "My daughter and I are both deeply sorry for that, too." She tried to catch Mr. Kalosoma's eye which had drifted over to Christina.

Mrs. Orony had invited Mr. Kalosoma for coffee and sweets. Sunday visit after church. Only more special today. Mr. Kalosoma looked to be uncomfortable in his funeral suit, now too tight. He pulled out a large kerchief from his pocket and held it to his brow.

"Yes. I'm very sorry to hear of Mr. Orony's death," he said, as Mrs. Orony set a cup of coffee in front of him.

"Thank you for your sentiments," Mrs. Orony said. "I certainly appreciate your inviting me here this afternoon to talk about our arrangement," he said, glancing at Christina and shearing off a thick piece of the cake slice Mrs. Orony had also placed before him.

Christina watched as Mr. Kalosoma swallowed a forkful without chewing.

"I have heard many good things about your daughter," he said, clearing his throat and nodding toward Christina.

"I would hope so," said Mrs. Orony. "There are many good things to say about her."

"Yes, yes," Mr. Kalosoma said hurriedly. "Here is something I want to give you." He leaned back in his chair, felt into a vest pocket and pulled out an old photograph folded in half to fit there. "This is me and my wife Eleni on our wedding day," he said, crossing himself. He passed it to Mrs. Orony who passed it on to Christina.

"You see, Christina, how beautiful Mrs. Kalosoma was," Mrs. Orony said. Then, turning to Mr. Kalosoma, adding, "And how is Mrs. Kalosoma doing, if I may ask?"

"The same," he said. "Always the same. And that's the miracle. She's still beautiful." He sighed, crossed himself again, and repeated: "A miracle."

He took off his glasses and squeezed the bridge of his nose with his thumb and forefinger.

"We are glad to hear that, Mr. Kalosoma. Very glad," Mrs. Orony said. "We are glad to hear that, aren't we, Christina?"

Christina nodded. "Yes, we are, Mama."

"You see, Mr. Kalosoma," Mrs. Orony said, sitting herself tall, placing her hands in her lap and interlacing her fingers. "Christina knows of your wife and her suffering, and she wants to be of help to you. She will be very good with your wife, Mr. Kalosoma. Your wife couldn't be in better hands than with Christina."

Mrs. Orony took a deep breath and looked from Mr. Kalosoma to Christina.

Mr. Kalosoma was pleased to follow her glance there, too. He sheared off another piece of Mrs. Orony's cake, and ate the frosting off it while the two women sat quietly.

"Yes, I'm sure," he said, putting his fork down and running his hand over his head. "I'm sure that Christina will do just fine."

"Do you hear that, Christina?" Mrs. Orony beamed. "You'll do just fine."

Christina nodded. She was still holding the wedding photograph of Mr. and Mrs. Kalosoma. She had held it out to her mother, then to Mr. Kalosoma, but neither would take it from her.

"No, no, Christina," Mr. Kalosoma finally said, shaking his head. "That's for you. That's for you to keep."

"Isn't that nice of Mr. Kalosoma, Christina," Mrs. Orony said. "That's a very special photograph he has given you."

Christina nodded and looked again at the photograph.

"Well," Mrs. Orony said with an air of finality as she got on her feet. "I'm sure that Christina is just what you and your wife will need. I believe that everything is set now."

Mr. Kalosoma cleared his throat, and remained seated. "I need to say something to you, Mrs. Orony, if I may," he said, looking up at her. "In front of this jewel, Christina." He lowered his head slightly in Christina's direction. "I wouldn't want to believe that I was depriving you of your daughter's services. I could not take her for Mrs. Kalosoma if I were depriving you in any way, Mrs. Orony. Not for a minute." He took Mrs. Orony's hand and kissed it lightly while his eyes ran over Christina. "Not for a minute," he said.

"Oh. No. No. Not at all," said Mrs. Orony, "So nice of you to worry about depriving me, Mr. Kalosoma. No, don't you worry about that at all, not one bit, do you hear?"

"All the same, gracious lady," Mr. Kalosoma persisted. "You need to know that I understand these matters." Glancing again at Christina, he dabbed his throat with his kerchief.

"Indeed you do, Mr. Kalosoma, indeed you do. And Christina here needs a situation, and her taking care of Mrs.

Kalosoma in her illness would be perfect for her. Isn't that right, Christina?"

"Yes, Mama, it is." Christina said as she looked down again at the photograph and ran her fingers over it.

"Best not to do that too much, darling," admonished Mrs. Orony. "It's an old photograph and will not last many more years if you run your fingers over it."

Christina looked up. "She's very beautiful, Mama, isn't she?"

Mrs. Orony took her hand and helped her to her feet. As she did so, Christina dropped the photograph. Mrs. Orony quickly picked it up, kissed it, and handed it back to her. Christina held it tightly to her chest as Mrs. Orony led her to Mr. Kalosoma, who was still seated. He had eaten the last of the frosting off the cake before him and was now free to address the two women. Thrusting his arms forward to leverage his weight, he rocked himself to his feet and stood before them.

"Well," he said, placing one hand on Christina's shoulder. "I'm sure you'll get on with Mrs. Kalosoma just fine."

Christina instinctively pulled back. Mrs. Orony squeezed her hand reassuringly.

"Good," said Mrs. Orony to both of them. "Everything is settled, then. I have all of Christina's things packed and ready. Isn't that right Christina?"

"Do I have to go right now?" Christina asked.

"Of course, child," said Mrs. Orony, "Mrs. Kalosoma is waiting for you."

She squeezed Christina's hand again and turned to Mr. Kalosoma. "Christina is a home girl, Mr. Kalosoma, and this arrangement is new to her. She's very shy as you can see."

Mr. Kalosoma studied Christina's face. "Of course, of course, she is," he said. "Of course she is." He looked at his watch, then at Christina. "Come now, sweet one, Mrs. Kalosoma is waiting for you."

Mrs. Orony came up to her. "You will need to go now, dear Christina. Mrs. Kalosoma is waiting for you."

"Can I bring Mrs. Kalosoma here to our house, Mama?"

"Maybe for a visit, dear, but not right away."

Daphne and the Mockingbird

T he first thing you noticed were the flowers. Hanging over us from a trellis, dripping nectar and pollen dust and dwarfing us as we sipped gin, only an hour till dinner, late afternoon in the corner of Daphne's densely planted courtyard, we sat at a glass-topped garden table with fertilizer bags on it, my wife and I, and Daphne, our hostess.

"David will be back in two days," Daphne said, "and I want to look pretty for him." She paused, took another sip of gin, leaned back in her chair for an instant, then forward again to place her elbows on the glass table top and whimper, "Look at me."

"What is it, Daphne?" my wife asked as she reached over to comfort her, a gesture Daphne seemed oblivious to as she pulled back, tilted her face forward, and muttered softly, "Look at these. Look at these dark circles under my eyes. That's what David will see, and I so want to look pretty for him."

And indeed, I could see that the circles under her eyes were more than their usual shade of speckled brown, looking now more like the undersides of dying leaves, not what she wanted David to see when she greeted him back from his business trip.

"These circles are from lack of sleep," she exclaimed emphatically, that it was that which had darkened her eyes and not the gin, telling us she couldn't sleep what with the nightly caw of a mockingbird that had settled in her magnolia tree. It had become her enemy.

"It sits up there somewhere...everywhere," she said, waving one hand at the twisted network of magnolia branches that canopied most of her courtyard. "Every night. Can you believe it? Every night! Just look at me." She was visibly trembling. My wife again reached over to comfort her, but as she did so, Daphne pulled her hand back, saying, "But don't you worry. My neighbor's going to take care of it."

"How?" I asked.

"With a BB gun," she said, "He's going to do it with a BB gun." Her voice quickening, she added, "He's going to sleep here in the courtyard, wait for it, and when he hears it, pow!" she exclaimed with a slap on the table. "Pow!"

"When?" I asked, somewhat discomfited by her plan. "As soon as it caws, sometime during the night," she said emphatically. "Sometime during the night. That's when it caws." She laughed nervously and put her hand over her mouth, as if she had said too much and feared that, in her excitement, she might appear odd to us.

The three of us sat silent for a moment, my wife and Daphne staring numbly at each other while I poured myself another glass of gin.

"How do you know it's a mockingbird?" I asked, finally. "I saw it!" she said stridently. "It's a mockingbird all right. I saw it!"

"Then it's not a caw," I said. "If it's a mockingbird, then what you heard was the night song of a male mockingbird singing for a mate. That's what you're hearing. There's nothing caw-like about it. It's melodious."

"Don't tell me what I'm hearing," she protested, angrily, as she took another sip of gin, "It's caw-like enough to keep me awake."

She paused and looked at us, as if to see if we stood with her on this. "Look, I'm against killing birds or any of God's creatures as much as either of you, but here I make an exception," she said, pointing at the overhanging branches of the magnolia tree. "I have to. That bird keeps me awake at night. Look at these!" She pressed her glass over a puffy lower lid, "I look like David's mother, not his wife. It's just that I need some sleep."

My wife and I exchanged glances, worried about what we'd heard. Daphne was an old friend, so was David her husband, and we'd never seen her as distraught as this. And what about the poor bird, I thought. Weren't there laws about killing birds? I wondered what her neighbor must be like to have agreed to killing one for Daphne.

I looked up into the tangle of magnolia branches, an attractive place for a mockingbird to build a nest for a mate once it had attracted one. How would it know this was Daphne's house, and about David, and about her needing to look good for him?

"I'm sorry but I still think it's a shitty thing to do, Daphne," I said finally. I saw instantly see that I shouldn't have said that, for she suddenly got very fidgety, so much so that she had to put her glass down and hold her arms tightly over her breasts, rocking back and forth as if to calm herself.

"Sure, I'm a little crazy right now," she said haltingly. "Forgive me." Then with a sudden change of tone, she added, "I'm so glad the two of you have come here for dinner. It should be ready about now." She shook her head as if to clear her thoughts, looked at my wife for an instant, took a deep breath, put her hands in my wife's lap, palms up, and rested her head on them.

"His name's Kenneth, my neighbor," she whimpered, as she raised her head to look at each of us, then to look back down at her hands. "His name's Kenneth. He'll be by soon to check the tree, to figure out how he's going to do it. He's very methodical." Her voice trailed off, then resumed in a whisper: "When he comes by, don't say anything about this please, it would embarrass him." She had a faraway look, maybe thinking how she'd look rested when David came home. Neither my wife nor I said a word.

I didn't think David would care much how she looked. David had a lady in another town, the one he'd gone to on his business trip, a long-term lady friend Daphne knew about her and my wife did too, we all knew that there was more wrong there than killing a bird would set right. But I knew how she was thinking, the darkness in her face, and still wanting to look good.

Maybe it was the gin that got me to blurt out about little Bobby, my age then, maybe eight or nine, walking into the courtyard of our tenement, a barren courtyard compared with this, walking into that courtyard with his BB gun soldier-like, owning the world for that moment, taking aim at a bird on a wire perch to see if he could hit it, and he did, then finding it on the ground broken and quivering, not quite dead, that was the worst of it, that it was not quite dead for so long a time that it made Bobby shake with what he'd done, quivering like that quivering bird, leaning over to touch it, to comfort it, to close the little red hole in its neck, waiting for it to die so he could bury it, and finally did, in a cigar box, like a person, laid out in there on a bed of twigs, a bird casket was how he thought of it, and he talked of it for days, that he had had no idea, none at all, about how it would be.

That memory, long silent, had awakened in me in a rush, which I regretted.

My wife glowered at me as Daphne lay her head back down on my wife's lap. "How could you tell a story like that!" my wife shrieked at me, then turned to Daphne and added, "I don't even think it's true, Daphne," she said, "He's making it up!"

Daphne sat up abruptly, shaking her head and pulling her hair back. "Kenneth said that he'd take the body away once he'd killed it so I wouldn't have to look at it." She suddenly stood up from the table, erect and looking resolved. "Excuse me," she said, "Be back in a minute. Got to see how the dinner's doing."

Daphne's leaving us even for a minute would have been welcome, but not now, as it left me alone with a very angry wife who was pointedly looking away from me, letting me know that I had said a bad thing.

I pushed back on my chair to create some distance between myself and my wife, bumping my head into a tangle of hanging blossoms, jarring loose pollen dust into my gin, which I downed and looked away from her. The only untroubled view left to me was of the magnolia tree. I found myself looking up at its boughs, wondering where in all this vast network of branches that poor bird would return to its favored place, alight, sing for its mate, and be shot.

When Daphne returned to sit down with us, my wife took Daphne's hands in hers to reassure her, the two of them ignoring me as I reached out from under the canopy of plants and flowers to seize my wife's unprotected gin, and downing that one too.

Daphne was an artist. Her smaller paintings very visible throughout her house, and her larger ones lining the walls of the sheltered parts of her courtyard. These were giant paintings of twisted trees and flowering plants, each the height of Daphne, painted in sweeping reds and greens, exaggerated and hyper-real, merging in form and color with the plants and trees in her courtyard, and with her.

From my exile and clouded a bit by the gin, I felt free to study her, and saw her as a large woman who gave the impression of having once been other than she was now, perhaps even beautiful, that her present appearance and manner were only temporary, even fleeting, and that she was, on balance, fictional.

My reverie was suddenly broken as the outside door to our floral enclosure swung open, and he stood before us in camouflage fatigues with a BB gun strapped onto his shoulder with a dog leash. I didn't have to be told that it was Kenneth, Daphne's neighbor. I had two thoughts, almost simultaneously, one that he was kidding, and the other that he wasn't. In either case I was glad that I was drinking. Daphne stood up and made introductions.

I stood up too and reached out to shake his hand. "Excuse me," he said, without offering his, and walked over to Daphne's tree as if pressing business was at hand. He stopped before it, tapped its trunk with his knuckles and to my surprise, began climbing it, eventually disappearing among its branches and leaves.

I looked over at Daphne for some sign that she had anticipated this but was put off by my wife's expression again. We all sat quietly waiting to see what would happen next, what Kenneth's next move might be. "Is he all right up there?" my wife asked, which Kenneth must have heard, for he shouted down from his perch, "Just go ahead, don't mind me, I'm setting myself up here. When that bird comes, I'll be ready."

I leaned over to Daphne, whispering so that Kenneth wouldn't hear, "From what you say, Daphne, that might not be for hours. Is he planning on being up there all night? Is he all right?" And to make the point I pointed to my head, which got me another dark look from my wife. Daphne got up without answering me. "Dinner's ready by now," she said, and led us into her dining room.

I struggled throughout dinner not to mention Kenneth being out there in her magnolia tree and that killing birds was probably illegal. Afterward, we returned to the courtyard for coffee and took our old seats at the garden table. It was dark now and Daphne brought out a large candle, which she placed atop one of the fertilizer bags. As I watched the flickering shadows the candlelight played against the plants surrounding us, there could be no mistake about it. Kenneth was snoring in the tree. He must have fallen asleep though I couldn't imagine how he was managing that in that tangle of branches.

It must have happened when he tried to change positions up there, to shift his weight, perhaps our voices after dinner in the garden again that might have startled him, but he fell to the ground, maybe ten feet, in a shower of leaves and small branches, stood up and claimed he was not hurt, though clearly stunned, for he seemed to be unsure exactly how he had ended up on the ground, indeed unsure of where he was just then. I thought perhaps he was still in whatever he had been dreaming while up in the tree. He made his way unsteadily to the trunk of the tree, stood before it for an instant, and then gave it a light karate chop as if challenging it to another match with him. Without a word, he then turned and went out the gate of the courtyard. I looked up and saw his BB gun hanging in the tree, held there by the dog leash.

When we got back home that night my wife still wouldn't speak to me, as if what had occurred there was my doing. We never spoke of it again.

Peter G. Tripodes

Millie's New Man

My wife and I were invited for drinks at Millie's and argued most of the way there. "I don't understand why she made Roger move out," I said, "I thought they were a great couple."

That triggered the expected response from Susan: "He was suffocating her, or didn't you notice? A real control freak, that Roger. She did right to get rid of him. A great couple, my foot!" Her voice had an air of finality and we didn't exchange another word for the rest of the trip.

I had always found Roger lively and entertaining and was certainly not now looking forward to a dull evening at Millie's, as it would be without him.

When we pulled up to Millie's, I found it depressing not seeing Roger's car in the drive. It had been maybe two months now, but this was the first time we'd been here since she had made him move out. I wouldn't have come were it not for Susan's shrill insistence that it was important that we be supportive of Millie now that she was alone. Susan had a way of intoning the word "alone" which she reserved for unattached women, which I found excessive here since it had been Millie who had forced Roger out.

As we walked up to the door of the house, Susan broke the silence: "She's an old friend, Tom, try to understand, and she needs to know that we haven't forsaken her, that's all. Don't you say anything hurtful to her. She's vulnerable right now."

I nodded and held my breath as I ran my hand across the door chimes, which tonight sounded grimly funereal as I awaited a tearful, hand wringing matron to greet us, and was happily surprised at Millie's appearance and demeanor. She was ebullient and girlish, not at all of her late-forty-some years, and fairly gurgling as she greeted us in apparent delight. Her perfume, which I had never before noticed, seemed tonight overpowering, as if applied in an unaccustomed fashion to a new self, one less bounded, I supposed, and, in spite of her apparently up-beat presentation of herself, I found myself feeling sorry for her, as she seemed somehow clownish.

She took Susan's hand, with me following. "I have a secret," she said excitedly. "Let me fix some drinks first before telling you. Gin and tonics as usual? I think I still remember. I'll be a minute."

"Make mine a big one," I shouted after her.

Susan and I sat in our usual places in the living room as Millie went into the kitchen to prepare our drinks, a soft chair in one corner for me, a seat at one end of the couch for Susan where Millie would soon be joining her, and a rocker next to the couch facing me, which had always been Roger's seat and was now empty. I must have been looking in its direction when I became aware of Susan staring at me, her eyebrows raised, a silent warning that I was not to make any reference to Roger's not being here.

When Millie returned with our drinks and took her seat next to Susan on the couch, I half expected in a macabre way that her secret was that she was pregnant, which would have been not only startling but nothing in her situation to be exuberant about, and was relieved to hear it that it was nothing like that.

She had met someone.

"His name's Ralph," she said.

I took a sip of my drink and looked at Susan, to get her measure of the news and to follow her lead on what to say to Millie. But Susan pointedly looked away from me, took Millie's hands in her own, and looked intently at her, all of which effectively excluded me.

"I'm so happy for you, Millie. That's wonderful!" she exclaimed. "Who is it?"

"His name's Ralph. You don't know him," Millie said, glancing now at both of us, perhaps not wanting me to be left out, perhaps even valuing a male input on this. "His name's Ralph," she repeated, "I know him from work."

I could tell she was nervous, excited, or both, repeating his name like that, like a schoolgirl.

I wanted somehow to show Millie that I was trying to be open to a replacement for Roger, but inevitably put it in a way that irritated Susan. "How long has Ralph been in the picture?" I asked.

Susan, who was palpably in hair-trigger tension about what I might say anyway, burst out, "That's a horrible way to ask about Millie's new man. You're purposely trivializing something very important to her."

"That's all right, Susan," Millie said, "I'm sure Tom meant no harm in that," then, turning to me, added, "About three weeks, Tom. I've known Ralph for about three weeks. I met him at work."

"Three weeks," I repeated after her, thinking how Roger had not long been gone before Millie's new man got figured in. I drained my glass and raised it up to her: "Another one here, Millie, when you get a chance." She took my empty glass into the kitchen, leaving Susan and me alone again.

I avoided Susan's eyes while Millie was gone, thinking to postpone any unpleasantness at least until the ride home, when there would be plenty of time for it. I was grateful for Millie's return with our drinks.

I took two large swallows and sat back resolved to be silent while I sipped on the rest of it. With this second drink I was beginning to feel more relaxed and sociable, even slightly sleepy. "This is a nice drink you fixed for me, Millie. Thank you, but I think Susan's glass is empty now, too."

Susan placed her hand over her glass and shook her head, which I read as a signal for me to be careful.

"What do you hear from Roger?" I asked. I don't know exactly why I asked that just then, bringing Roger's name up, except perhaps from feeling that, after showing concern for Susan's drink, I had earned the right to mention Roger. After all, he wasn't dead or anything.

"Just the legal stuff," Millie answered flatly, "Nothing personal."

Susan broke in: "You don't have to answer any of Tom's stupid questions, Millie."

"That's OK, I don't mind," Millie said, graciously, and smiled slightly in my direction.

Not much encouragement, but enough. "It's good that you guys didn't have any kids," I broke in. "That would have complicated things."

Millie shook her head and looked tearful. I knew that she had always wanted children but had never had them. "Nothing like that," she said softly, and the two women exchanged glances, now at my expense.

Feeling increasingly marginalized, I felt driven to continue: "How are you guys dividing things up, anyway?" I asked, as if representing Roger's interest here in his absence.

"Good God, Tom!" Susan shrieked, "Have you no sense of things? It's none of your goddam business." Then turning to Millie, she held up her glass, "Thanks, I will have a bit more, say half-way to the top, but no more."

"Fill it to the top," I said loudly, trying to sound jovial as well as to implicate the drinks as partly responsible for my actions. "But none for me," I added with an air of restraint that I hoped might reinstate me with Susan. I nestled back in my soft chair and resolved to be quiet. I was getting sleepy anyway.

I must have dozed for a few seconds and woke up to the sound of their voices, which had become more animated.

"Ralph is real nice," Millie was saying to Susan, "You'll like him."

"I'm sure I would," Susan said, glancing over at me. I opened my eyes wide to show her I was fully awake now and should be included in whatever they were saying.

"He's very different from Roger," Millie went on. "He's everything that Roger isn't."

Hearing Roger now mentioned in a negative light alerted me, as I felt that I had to defend him. "What's that that Ralph is and Roger isn't?" I said, instantly regretting it.

"He listens," Millie said, meaningfully, with a clarity and pointedness that surprised me. I felt it an accusation, though perhaps unintentional.

"He does what?" I asked.

"She said that Ralph listens, Tom. Something Roger never did. Nor you."

"You don't have to spit that at me, Susan, I know what she means."

"I doubt it," Susan said, turning from me to face Millie and, in a gesture of schoolgirl intimacy, reached for her hands again, whispering, "Tell me about him."

"Yes, tell us how he listens," I yelled, in spite of my resolve not to speak. I was feeling my drinks and could plead intoxication if worse came to worst.

"Don't be cute, Tom," Susan scowled. "There's something you could learn about listening, too. If you'd just shut up once in a while."

I drew my finger over my lips, reached over to a side table to pick up a magazine.

Before I could open it, Millie interrupted, "I have a surprise, you two. You can put down that magazine, Tom. Now listen to my surprise: I've invited Ralph to join us here tonight so the two of you could meet him."

"Here? When?" I stammered, sensing the door closing on any claim Roger might yet have here.

Millie looked at her watch. "He'll be here any minute now," she said excitedly. "He's coming to join us now for drinks! I thought it would be a good chance for you to get to know him. What do you think?"

I instinctively raised my glass to Millie for a refill but just then the door chimes rang. "I'll be back to fix your drink, Tom, but let me get the door first. I think it must be Ralph. He's very punctual."

As she opened the door, Susan and I stood up. It was awkward, but we stood up, perhaps in my case to show someone who was not wholly welcome that he was, and with me a bit wobbly, it took some effort to stand without wavering as he walked in. I wondered if he would notice and think me odd.

"This is Ralph," Millie said, as she walked him in with her arm under his, then gesturing toward us with the other arm, added, "Susan and Tom, here." Ralph shook Susan's hand, saying, "You're Susan," then shook mine, saying, "You're Tom," which struck me as peculiar, maybe even a bit retarded, like a child memorizing names of grown-ups he was meeting.

Ralph, happily, seemed so innocent that it relaxed me a bit and I hesitated to say anything even remotely unpleasant, or even surprising. Since Susan's threshold for what she could not take from me was dangerously low, I waited for Millie to develop social openers. But as she seemed fully absorbed in Ralph for the moment, I felt I had to speak.

"Can we sit down now?" I asked, feeling unsteady on my feet.

"Of course we can," Millie said, beckoning us all to sit. She motioned Ralph to take Roger's old seat, the rocker, which I felt he had no right to.

Once seated, I felt renewed. At least enough to ask Ralph, "Where did you two meet?" already a stupid question since Millie had already twice said that she knew Ralph from work. But he answered anyway. "From work," he said. "I knew Millie from work." So that was that.

"Yes," Millie. elaborated, "but it wasn't like we really knew each other at work. Ralph worked in accounting, which is far from the reception desk where I work. It was at an office party three weeks ago that we really got to know each other."

"Yes," Ralph chimed in, "The rest is history."

"What history?" I asked. It was a real question, but worded after an old habit from college, exposing the misuse of an idiom, here inadvertently and at Ralph's expense, which I instantly regretted, especially since it got me another dark look from Susan.

"He means to ask," Susan broke in, "what happened from that point on between the two of you? How did your relationship develop?"

Ralph's face clouded. "Some of that's personal," he said, which made me miss Roger again. I couldn't believe Ralph had actually said that and felt vindicated for my low expectations of the evening.

"Maybe you can tell us about the non-personal part, then," I persisted. Susan knew how I meant that, that it was an unanswerable request, that anything that Ralph could say then would sound foolish. And she would punish me later for it.

"I can tell you what's personal, if it's all right with Ralph," Millie said, looking over at Ralph for his approval.

"Do you mind," I broke in, "I sort of wanted to hear Ralph out on this, if that's OK with him, whatever part he wants to talk about."

Ralph looked quizzically at Millie, leaned over and whispered something in her ear. She looked back at me and announced that Ralph wanted her to tell the personal part for him.

I was disappointed that she chose to answer the question I had put to Ralph, as I was beginning to feel that Ralph had a way of putting things that might save an otherwise abysmally dull evening.

Millie drew herself up as she sat: "I had taken the lead with Ralph," she began, "asking him if he was married. He had said that was a personal question but that it might be all right for him to answer me since we both worked for the same company."

"He actually said that?" I asked, suppressing a smile as I took another hard look from Susan.

"Yes," Millie went on, "he did say that." Then she paused to look over at Ralph as if to see if it was all right with him if she continued. As he nodded, I broke in again, still feeling cheated of hearing about it in his own words: "What was personal about it?"

"Ralph had been married once before," she said, "It had been to his mother."

An eerie quiet settled over us till it was broken by Susan. "I can see why Ralph may have thought that that was personal." It surprised me that Susan could say that matter-of-factly, as if such a disclosure were commonplace.

"Of course, it's pretty clear now," I chimed in, seeking to be in agreement with Susan on something. "It's pretty clear why you might regard that as personal, Ralph. You certainly wouldn't say that to just anyone."

"It isn't what it sounds like," Ralph said, "It was my stepmother."

"Oh," Susan said, "That's different."

"Yes, very different," I agreed.

"His stepmother," repeated Millie. "She was really too old for him. That's why it didn't work out."

"Yes," Susan said. "One can certainly see how that would be. An age difference can be a big problem. May-December marriages are difficult."

"We were married in August," Ralph said.

"Yes, of course," I agreed, rather appreciating the various abrupt turns our conversation was taking, and feeling more and more connected with Ralph.

"How long did it last?" I asked. Millie didn't wait for Ralph to answer and broke in, "A week. They'd been married for just a week. You can't really call that a marriage."

"No, you can't," I added, in a redeeming effort to be agreeable.

"It was a summer romance," Ralph volunteered. "But the age difference was too much for us."

Ralph slowly got up from the rocker and walked over to the couch to stand in front of Millie, who remained seated next to Susan.

There was a gap of a few seconds, which I thought to fill in: "You can't trust summer romances," I said, "They sweep one off one's feet."

"Yes," Ralph said. "It wasn't working out. The age difference, you know." He took Millie's hand in his and smiled. "Millie here got me on the rebound."

That's when things turned a bit more bizarre as Ralph leaned over Millie and began to kiss the top of her head in a series of rapid kisses. I watched as Susan tried to lean away from them.

"Oh, stop that Ralph," Millie said in the girlish voice she had greeted us with when we had first come in, then turned to look at Susan.

"Ralph is very emotional," she said, blushing, as Ralph walked back to his rocker, then added, "Does Tom ever do that with you?"

"Sometimes," I lied, not wanting the bizarreness of the mood to dissipate.

"I would have guessed that," Ralph said, approvingly, came over to me and shook my hand.

Susan looked at me, and then smiled broadly. "Sometimes," she said. Her comment surprised and warmed me, the best I'd felt all evening.

"I'm sure of it," Ralph said. "I'm a pretty good judge of people, am I not, Millie?"

"Of course you are, Ralph," she said, then turning to us, added, "He is, you know."

"I am what?" Ralph asked.

"A good judge of people, Ralph."

"Yes, I am, and I'd say that you're a good judge of people too, Millie, to have friends like these," pointing first at Susan and then at me while announcing our names again.

"Let's hold hands on that," he said, reaching his out to us, which Susan and I, now of one mind, exchanged glances and took, albeit reluctantly.

I was grateful to Ralph for helping Susan and me come to this point, and I came increasingly to think better of him, even fondly, which surprised me, almost as of an innocent with a gift for healing. I wondered what Roger would have made of him, of this evening, and wondered how the evening would have gone if Roger were here instead. It passed my mind to call Roger the next day to fill him in on his replacement, but then I thought better of it.

On the way home, I asked Susan what she thought of Ralph and of the evening. "I don't know," she said, laughing. "I just don't know."

"Do you think Millie loves him?" I asked.

"I think she does," she said, then kissed her finger and touched it to my forehead.

Saying Goodbye

M ary said that I had to move out of her apartment that very day, that she couldn't believe that I did not know she had a lover, and that she couldn't respect me for that. She suggested that I might look for someone younger, less clever, someone maybe nineteen, and anyway I had to get out because there was no room for three. It happened very quickly.

I found a furnished basement room in the building next door, so close that I could see Mary's bathroom light at night when I looked up from my bed, but that was all that was good. It had a ceiling so low that I couldn't stand up, and though I took it, I don't see how anyone can rent you a room like that without worrying what you think. Mary would be embarrassed for me that I took it just to be nearby. I could press the palms of my hands to the ceiling when I sat up in bed. It felt like a tomb.

I didn't sleep at all that first night.

But the morning of my first day's release, the first morning I was out alone, the very first day out, sitting at the counter at Norm's having coffee and toast the first time feeling good about being free, being without Mary and all her talk, somewhat relieved, only two sips into my coffee I heard someone's teeth go ping. It was the girl sitting next to me, eating a breakfast roll, her fork hitting her teeth. She watched me watching her out of the corner of her eye, listening to her eat. Ping, ping, she did it again. This time for me, and laughed, again, louder than before, and I laughed too, turned fully to face her and then she to me blushing big-eyed through her bangs, didn't let up, did it even louder, facing me, pinging her teeth, and people looking at me, almost thirty and this sassy kid, plain as grass. I finally spoke, "How old are you?" and held my breath as she said, "Nineteen."

This was Jennie, freckled, big white teeth, looked like she'd grin and snap gum in bed. It turned out she did. I recalled that Mary had little teeth, and how for her sex was more a concept thing. I thought about that too.

I told Jennie about my room and how you couldn't stand up. She laughed and wanted to see. I knew she would. Some days you're on.

"You're kidding," I said, "It's five blocks away."

"Let's see it," she said, wild, like field air before rain.

"Are you sure?"

"Yes, I am," laughing again, and we went there and spent the day.

Everything with Jennie seemed so easy, so smooth, we laughed more than we talked, nothing meant anything more than it was, at least, that's the way it seemed.

But Jennie had to come from somewhere, like everyone else, at first just shadows, but then more, and it made her make trouble for me. Nothing really to do with me. She told me about her dad stumbling into the kitchen drunk, beating up her mom, backing off, shaking, her mom's brothers in reprisal, three of them, coming in to beat him up, running in yelling like to do murder, pounding and kicking her dad down flat, yelling they didn't care if he died, one getting up to tear off her blouse to see her breasts, while the others laughed, she was just fourteen. It got worse, she said, and whatever it was, it came back to make trouble for me.

She told me that her own boyfriends were boys, pretty, gentle, well-mannered boys, pink-nailed, dove-like, cooing boys, with soft, girl-like skin and hairless chests. She told me how she had found and married one—a figure skater full of grace, bird-like, smooth and effortless. "I didn't believe he was real," she said, "I didn't think a fellow could move like that." That was what she called him, "a fellow," she said. She would recall how she had watched him practice, how he was like a movie star for her, king of the rink. He'd be famous some day and take her away, how she wooed him and became his girl, wooed him some more and became his wife, then she told me in a whisper that quivered my ear, as we lay there sex-spent in my tomb of a bed, in a hot whisper that got me going again, that she couldn't love just him, that she missed something.

I could see where she might be trouble for me as she was for him, as Mary had been for me. I'd been here before.

So she was married. I wouldn't have guessed she looked so young. Maybe it was better that I only be her occasional guy, her real one waiting in their marriage bed, asking her, "Jennie, where have you been?" asking to hear her lies. Yes, I would be freer this way. You never know, Mary might come one day looking for me.

But Jennie would never leave my side, as we lay in that bed under the low ceiling, it was a tomb. "Don't you ever have to go home?" I asked. "Doesn't your husband ever need you there?"

"Why do you ask me things like that?" she said. "Don't you want to be here with me?" I felt her freckly soap scent all over me, talcum sweat sweet sticky, sticking to me, Jennie's scent filled the room, her legs locking around me and me to that bed, stop it don't make me die, Jennie, please go to sleep, and she'd sleep still locked onto me.

I could never get away, I began to think this kid is crazy, to feel ensnared, especially with more hot whispers about how she had gotten pregnant a couple of times and that it was too easy for her so that we had to be careful, which we of course we were not, not once, not ever, in that sweaty bed, so when she whispered her new secret just for me that she was pregnant again, and said that it had to be me, I felt too written in, too ensnared, and had to get out, no matter what.

I even began to miss Mary's concept talk, began to look for her bathroom light to come on, imagined her talking through the bathroom door to her lover while one or the other sat on the can, Mary talking about their relationship as if a separate thing, separate from them, with a life of its own, just as she used to do with me. I found myself wanting that again.

The crisis with Jennie turned out to be a false alarm. Her period came and I never wanted to touch her again, maybe I had thought to save her like everyone who ended up in the sack with her. Anyway, she wasn't quite what I thought, a little too off my regular feed, too bubble-gum horsey, clutching, and big boned for me.

Maybe Mary had spoiled me, Mary who had talked sex to a serious death that came in and went in a flood of words, incessant talking about what it meant, who we were, and all of that. Jennie more inclined to the physical end. I could never quite get used to it, sometimes banging my balls with her knees when she'd turn over in bed, I think just to hear me yell. And when the mood would seize her she'd jump on top, her head banging on my low ceiling light, straddle down hard on me with my prick inside, then lean back like a joke on me, get it to push to the front to make a bump on her belly to see for herself how it looked like to come right through, move the light to make the shadow of the prick bump clear, "My God, look at that!" Vaudeville fun for her and it made her laugh. I wondered if that's what was making her pregnant so much. Anyway, when it turned out she wasn't, I saw I was clear and we stopped everything. "That's it," I said, "I'm sorry," I said, "I can't see you again." She didn't cry, she unwrapped from me, sat up tall, naked and leaning forward, the low ceiling at her head, pushing the light bulb away from her hair, a smell of hair burning, she looked crippled and bent, staring at me like I'd hit her. The light in her was gone, she looked old, picked her things up hurriedly and went out into the street, half naked and seeming crazy.

Her next reaching back to me after that was a gentle one, not deserving of how I handled it. She had called me from the Greyhound bus station one night, two weeks later, said she was going back to Texas to live with an aunt, "Would you rather I didn't go?" she asked. When I said nothing she asked at least would I see her off.

"Sure," I said, then took my time getting there and just as the bus was taking off, to see her standing in the aisle stooping to see out the window if I'd come.

I waved but I don't know if she saw me.

The Girl from the Lunchroom

T his was the building she had described. Her apartment. The one on the lower left. Newspapers on the windows. No blinds or curtains yet, she'd said. Had just moved in. No mistake but that this was the place. Gary could hardly believe she had invited him.

He rang the bell. Then again. And waited.

He raised his scarf higher on the back of his neck, held it snugly under his ears with one hand, and tucked it in close to his throat with the other. With the damp evening air coming in he feared he'd become hoarse again.

Not to stand out too long if he could help it, he rang again. Yet, still no answer.

So why wasn't she answering? Gary stepped off the stoop to peer into a window, one where newspaper had separated from the window sash. Not much space to look through, though. From what he could see of it, the apartment looked empty, though in that fading light he could not see into it clearly. Somebody better answer soon. The cold was getting to him. He stepped back on to the stoop, squared himself at the doorbell and rang again.

"Oh, Jesus. Be here."

There was no answer.

There had been no empty tables in the lunchroom earlier that day and Gary had to look for someone to share theirs with him, someone sitting alone. He hated having to do this. To eat your lunch across from a stranger who would have preferred to eat alone. He saw a table at one end of the lunchroom. A young girl sitting alone, reading a magazine over a sandwich. He fought his shyness to ask her, a perfect stranger, if it was all right for him to sit at her table. "Hi," he asked hoarsely, "is this seat taken?"

She nodded without looking up, her attention on what she was reading. Gary felt invisible. He hated this lunchroom. And, for an instant, he hated this girl, too. She could at least have looked up at him.

He stared down at her numbly, at her black dress, simple and businesslike. Sleeveless, it exposed smooth, graceful arms and promised movement that was effortless. Gary was large and the tables in the lunchroom small and boutiquish. He felt his a potentially clumsy presence—that she would see him that way. He took a deep breath and looked off into the noisy lunchroom, as if still searching for another table so as not to trouble her. Then back to the girl, to her dark hair parted sharply down the middle, falling softly over her shoulders. She wasn't from the bank like most everybody else here. Gary would have remembered her.

"Yes, it's fine," she said, finally looking up at him. "I'm not expecting anyone," then turned back to her reading again.

"Thanks," he said, taking the seat across from her, wishing that his normal voice would return to him.

His throat had been bothering him all morning. It didn't help that he had to work under a ventilation grid at the bank. Whenever he'd move his desk away from it, someone would move it back again. So he had gotten to wearing a scarf at his desk, at first only when he felt a chill—but now, all the time, and everywhere. A chill seemed to follow him.

Even here, at this girl's table, he felt a draft. Even here. Gary scanned the ceiling to see if there was a ventilation grid over his head. There wasn't any that he could see, but he could swear he heard a fan somewhere.

Gary settled in his chair, tucked his scarf to his throat as he sat, looking about as if distracted, to look less the intruder, a smaller presence. He turned slowly to get both legs under the table, one knee slightly bumping the table. Not much room for a large man like Gary. He wouldn't be eating lunch here at all if it wasn't next to the bank. He hated this lunchroom.

He didn't have to look directly at her to figure that she was in her early twenties. Twenty-five on the outside. Gary didn't trust himself much anymore on guessing ages. Not since his divorce from Lorrie. This one was lots younger than Lorrie. Probably Lorrie's age when he had first met her. Hard to remember Lorrie ever looking this good, though.

Gary opened his newspaper, folded it crisply into quarters as if he had other things on his mind, and pressed it compactly to the table to read. His answer to her magazine. Both now hunched to their reading.

She must be going on a job interview, dressed that way. Too good for everyday. Gary glanced at her magazine, which he thought might be a fashion magazine of some sort. Whatever it was, it was opened to a page on plumbing. He could tell even looking at it upside down and from a distance.

Suddenly, a familiar grating voice. The waitress yelling, "I'll be there in a minute, honey!" She was yelling at him from the coffee urn, a long way off. She always did that to embarrass him. Gary always tried to avoid her tables. An accident that this girl had come to sit alone at one of them.

Gary stared down at his folded newspaper as the waitress, coming closer, yelled again. "Lift your paper to see the menu, honey!" Gary lifted his newspaper and glanced at the menu printed on a plastic placemat in front of him. Instinctively, he looked up to see what the girl was having. He never ordered before he saw what someone else had ordered. Lorrie had always hated that about him.

"Is that good?" he asked the girl, as if she were Lorrie. As if he knew her. His own voice sounded weak and unfamiliar to him, like that of a consumptive who had not eaten a real meal for a while. And deranged enough to mistake a stranger for someone he knew.

"What?"

He had almost forgotten what he'd asked her. She was looking directly at him now, and it flustered him.

"Your sandwich," he said finally. No question about it. His throat was worse.

"I don't know. I haven't touched it," she said, absently, turning back to her magazine, but now glancing at him occasionally.

Gary had gotten so tense that he didn't really feel much like eating. Didn't much feel like being here either. It reminded him of when he and Lorrie were talking divorce over lunch and she would be reading a magazine instead of talking. She had already erased him from her world. Read that magazine as if she were eating alone. Going through the motions of being a couple. "I don't know who you are, anymore." Lorrie would say that all the time near the end. He had some of that feeling here too.

He wondered if the girl was attached to anyone. If she was somebody's Lorrie. Already erasing men from her life. Even strangers like him. She was better looking than Lorrie who had lost some of her looks while married to him. Lorrie didn't take much care of herself near the end. And this one was younger.

No rings except for one on her right index finger—a new-age band of some sort. Anyway, it said that she was single. No lockets, no jewelry. No markers of choices made by her or for her. He remembered Lorrie's heavy jewelry and perfumes. This one so different—in a simple black dress and casually falling hair. Gary liked that. And pretty. Very much so.

She looked up again and caught him staring. She smiled at him easily, and it relaxed him. A little.

"Plumbing," she said off-handedly, acknowledging that Gary had noticed what she was reading, and that he had probably thought it unusual for a girl to be interested in that.

"Yes, I can see that," he said, as matter of factly as he could, as if it was no surprise to him.

She smiled with her explanation: "I have leaky pipes in my apartment."

"I work at the bank." Gary felt dumb coming back with that.

"I know," she said. "I've seen you there. In the back. In the last desk by the wall. You're very isolated."

Gary hated his job more than ever.

The shadow of the waitress fell over them. "OK, I'm here," she announced. What'll you have, honey?"

"I don't know yet," Gary said, irritably. He didn't want to deal with the waitress, conscious now also that the girl was listening. So she had seen him in the bank. Shivering under a ventilation grid. She had probably noticed that, too. That was awful. Gary fingered his scarf.

"We don't have all day, honey," the waitress said, shifting her weight from foot to foot. Always overly familiar and gruff, she leaned over Gary and tapped her check pad on the plastic menu in front of him.

"Choose one, honey, anyone. Be a sport and order. I've got other tables, too."

She knew he was shy and was making fun of him, making him look like a fool in front of this girl.

"I'll have one of those," he said, pointing to the sandwich on the girl's plate.

"OK," she said, and yelled it across the lunchroom. "Another ham and cheese on rye."

Gary looked back at the girl and was surprised to find her looking directly at him. "Do you know anything about plumbing?" she asked, a new earnestness about her. And a new interest in him.

"Some," he said, worried that he may have overstated it.

"Do you have a pipe wrench?" she asked.

Gary thought it was a test. To see if he knew enough about plumbing to have a pipe wrench.

"I can get one," he said.

"That's terrific!" she said, with a surprising burst of enthusiasm. "I have most everything else." She suddenly sounded like a schoolgirl, wholly unselfconscious. She reached into her purse and pulled out a business card with only her name and address on it. No telephone number. No business. Nothing.

"Would you come by, or could you, to give me a hand with this?"

"Sure. When?"

"How about this evening. After five. Anytime after five."

"Sure."

She wrote out directions on the back of the card, then looked up at Gary, and said with tutorial clarity, which pleased Gary: "The apartment on the lower left. You'll see the newspapers covering all the windows. You can't miss the place." She had said it the way Lorrie would have. That had been the best part of Lorrie. Giving directions.

"Thanks," the girl said, getting up for her chair, and adding, "I'll expect you," as she left. Gary looked across at her plate and saw that she had never touched her sandwich.

Gary rang again. This time pressing it a long time. If she's asleep, this will wake her, he thought.

At last he could hear footsteps approaching. The door opened and she stood there. Just as she had been in the lunchroom. But that was all that was familiar. She seemed disoriented and did not appear to recognize him.

"From the lunchroom," Gary reminded her, holding up his pipe wrench. He felt he should have been holding up a menu too. "This afternoon. At the lunchroom. I'm the one from the bank. At the last desk."

She looked at him for a moment. Gary guessed that she'd been napping.

"Oh, yes, it's you. You'd better come in," she said, but this time without enthusiasm. The pipe wrench not a big deal anymore. Nor he.

Gary stepped in and found himself in an empty apartment. A large living room and two smaller rooms opening from it that he could see. And newspapers everywhere. They covered all the windows and were strewn about on the floor, haphazardly covering it. Some piled in the corner, wet and matted. Something to do with the plumbing leaks.

The air in the apartment was pungent with the smell of wet newspaper.

"I'm trying to fix the place," she said, as if sleepwalking.

"Are you all right?" Gary asked.

She nodded.

"Do you live here, now?" he asked.

"Yes," she said, reviving somewhat at the question. "It's nice except for the leaks."

It didn't seem very nice to Gary. It was as cold inside as out. This was a good place to get sick. Even more than he was already.

"Why do you keep it so cold in here?" he asked.

"There's no heat. That's my next problem. But I've got to get the leaks fixed first."

"Aren't you cold?" he asked. She was still in her sleeveless dress.

"I'm used to it."

Gary wasn't. Maybe they could go somewhere warmer. He thought to suggest that to her. Maybe a restaurant. Maybe his place. It was much nicer in the lunchroom. Even that.

As if reading his mind, she said, "I can't leave here. Not till I fix some things. I can't leave it like this."

"You mean the plumbing leaks?"

"Yes," she said. "Come see how the floors are getting ruined."

She took his hand. It was the first time they touched. And it was she who touched him. Her hand was like ice.

"Come with me," she said, leading Gary into one of the two rooms that opened from the large entry room. Water was oozing out of the ceiling in dozens of droplet streams. She pulled him through the room as water sprinkled over them. Gary felt wet through and through, though it was mainly his scarf he was concerned about. It was wet now, too. And his throat felt worse.

"This room isn't as bad as another room here," she said, adding, "Come with me," as she pulled him into a second room.

Gary found water streaming down one of the walls in sheets, and onto the floor where it had been dammed up by newspapers piled knee high at its base. They were saturated and clearly could not hold back any more water, which was beginning to flow along the floor and into the other room.

"Did you bring your wrench with you?" she asked.

It seemed preposterous to expect much from it, but Gary showed her that he had not forgotten to bring it, not at all sure what he'd do with it here.

"Good," she said. "Could you get started on this now? Things are getting pretty awful." She seemed fully awake now.

For an instant, Gary hoped it was a joke—that she was trashing this place and wanted him to come in on it with her. He would have hoped that, but it wasn't so. He quickly saw in her eyes that she was desperate. No mistake about that.

This was more than he could handle, by lots. And his throat. Gary was getting soaked in here. And he was freezing. His only thought now was to get away.

But first, to make some sense of this girl's dilemma, to make a transitioned exit.

"How long have you lived here?" he asked, trying for a measured, problem-solving tone.

"I moved in this morning, just before I met you in the lunchroom. I was hoping you could help me with this. It wasn't so bad this morning."

"It's plenty serious now," Gary interrupted. "Your landlord needs to handle this. Get him on the phone."

"I don't have one. Besides, I'm supposed to be managing this and the other units myself. I'm to live here rent free so long as I keep the units in good shape and collect the rents."

"But it's in terrible shape. At least yours is. He can't have you come in with leaks like this! Are the other apartments any better?"

"I don't know. I just started."

Gary would leave at the next opening. If there wasn't one, he'd make one. For the moment, better to appease her. He began to studiously tap at the wall with his pipe wrench, more to be doing something than to any purpose. Like tapping a wall. And the girl seemed momentarily pleased that he was doing something about the problem.

That tapping was all the wall needed. It bulged out in a big blister at the point where Gary had tapped it and suddenly let go. A torrent of water flowed into the room, out through the doorway and into the other room.

"You shouldn't have done that," she shrieked. "You've got water everywhere now!"

"It was inevitable," he said, trying to reason with her. "The whole place is going to cave in. It was in the works, from the beginning."

She began to tremble. Gary instinctively reached out his arms to hold her, to comfort her. She leaned on his shoulder and began to cry.

"Please don't cry. It'll work out," Gary said mindlessly, still thinking how to exit himself from this scene. It was out of control and no way for him to even begin to handle it. And so was she. No way there either. Gary could not imagine her ever being normal again even if she and the apartment got dried out thoroughly. His image of her at the lunchroom seemed very remote.

She sensed what he was thinking, to get out, and suddenly jerked back and stared at him. Her eyes were wild, and scanned him savagely. Then screamed in a voice that could have shattered glass: "You're not going to leave! No! You can't! I need you to help me! Pleased don't leave."

"I won't leave," Gary said, while planning to, "but you've got to calm down. Please."

Suddenly, the girl brightened. She stepped back from him, splashing water about her ankles as she moved, and kicked off her wet shoes, laughing.

"Don't think me crazy, please," she pleaded, "promise you won't think me crazy." Her voice was playful and imploring.

Gary thought of Lorrie and felt paralyzed. Lorrie wouldn't be like this.

The girl drew her dress off her, up over her head in one graceful move and tossed it to the floor, where it bubbled up then floated flat in a full inch of water. As Gary followed the trail of the dress she began to dance before him in her bra and panties, her skin blue from the cold, her lips tight and grim.

Gary was freezing. Water had soaked his trousers almost to the knees and he was dreadfully cold. Gary thought of Eskimos having sex in igloos, this the seduction dance. His only thought here was to leave.

He stood limply before her, a silent audience to her eccentricities, mesmerized by it all somehow, wondering how it would end, when suddenly, she sprang up at him, as if finishing something begun of which he was not aware, clasped him with her legs and arms like an infant chimpanzee. Gary could hardly maintain his balance. Instinctively, he tried to peel her off.

"You can't leave me, you know," she said, touching her nose to his. "I won't let you. You won't, will you. You don't even want to go now, do you? Not really."

"I won't go yet, but you'll have to get down." Gary lied. "Please."

The girl leaped off him, ran to the front door and bolted it. She spread herself across the door, facing him, her arms stretched out on either side.

"Thou shall not pass!" she laughed. "Come. Try to."

Suddenly, a shadow crossed her face, and her mouth sagged as if she had been struck. Still spread across the door, she shook her head violently, her hair flying from side to side. "I don't want you here!" she screamed.

"OK. Let me get out, then." She abruptly turned, unbolted the door and moved aside, but just as Gary stepped toward it, she jumped onto him again, this time knocking him to the floor.

"I knew it!" she screamed.

Gary managed to writhe himself free, stood up with a jerk, and ran out the door.

"Why are you leaving?" she shouted after him. "I thought you had come to help me."

He wasn't surprised the next day to see her in the bank, staring at him at his desk in back. She had staked out a vigil there. He thought waiting for lunchtime. She looked amazingly composed. He, of course, had lost his voice completely now, and hoped he wouldn't have to explain anything.

Park Bench

He threw his coat over the back of the bench and sat down next to her. "Are you a nurse?" he asked.

"No."

"You look like a nurse."

"Well, I'm not," she said.

He unwrapped a sandwich. "Do you mind if I eat this?" he asked.

She didn't answer him.

"You sure you're not a nurse, miss?"

She shook her head without looking at him.

"That's OK with me," he said, "It doesn't matter to me if you're a nurse or not."

"That's good," she said flatly, drawing a letter out of her purse, unfolding it and beginning to read.

"Excuse me, miss, I just want to say I'm sorry to have bothered you." He shook his head and took a bite of his sandwich. "I didn't mean to interrupt you."

She didn't answer him.

He watched her as she read her letter, then broke in again.

"Would you like the other half of this sandwich?" he asked, holding his offering to her. "Too much for me here," then paused, to add: "It's very good."

"No," she said, not looking back at him.

"I'll have to throw this half away, then, if you don't want it. Too much for me, here. Pity to waste it, though."

She turned and looked at him blankly, then turned back without saying a word.

"You're sure you're not a nurse, then, miss?" he asked.

"Well, I'm not," she said, folding the letter and placing it back in her purse, then added, without looking at him: "Why do you keep asking me that? Are you a doctor?"

"As a matter of fact, I am," he said.

"Well, you don't look like a doctor to me."

"Believe what you want," he said.

"Well thanks for that!" she said, raising her collar and pulling the sleeves of her coat down over her hands.

"It's cold, isn't it?" he said. "You were always cold in the hospital, complaining about not having enough heat. You were right of course. They always keep it on the cool side."

"That's ridiculous," she exclaimed, finally turning to look at him. "I don't remember seeing you there. To say nothing of talking to you about the heat."

He studied the remains of his sandwich, then looked up. "Well. I remember you."

"You've confused me with someone else," she said, tightening her fingers over the latch of her purse.

"I don't think so," he said, as he took another bite of his sandwich. "No. I'm quite certain that I remember you."

"Are you on medication?" she asked.

"You have no call to ask that," he said. "I didn't mean to trouble you. I was just making conversation on my lunch break."

"It didn't sound like that to me."

"What did it sound like to you?" he asked.

"Like you were prying."

"Oh, good heavens," he exclaimed, drawing a sandwich crumb from his lip with his finger, examining it for an instant before eating it. "Prying? No. I wouldn't do that. Wouldn't think of it."

"Well, what was all that about then?" she asked, "going on and on about my being a nurse?"

"It was just a question, a natural one, given your clothing, your uniform, and these being the hospital grounds. It's a nurse's uniform, isn't it? I'd know one when I see one. And besides, I think I saw you on the wards once or twice."

"Well, whoever you saw, it wasn't me," she said.

"No," he said, "I'm sure of it. I would remember any nurses who work around me. We're a community there, as you should know. And I remember you."

"No, I don't think so," she said.

He shook his head, gazing downward. "I'm sure of it."

She took a long look back at him. "You were a patient there, weren't you?" she asked.

"Hardly," he said, raising his hand. "Let me get this last bite down." He quickly chewed and swallowed what was left of his sandwich and turned to her. "No," he said, "Not a patient. Hardly."

She sat quietly, studying him. "I remember you now," she said. "You were on the third floor ward, weren't you?"

"I may have had rounds there, that is certainly possible, and probably that is where you had seen me and where I had seen you. You see, you do remember seeing me at the hospital, as I said."

"No, not quite like you said, sir. You were strapped to your bed."

"Good heavens, madam" he exclaimed, bursting into laughter. "You've got some real confusion there. I hope you're dealing with it."

She shook her head and folded her arms, nesting her hands under them as if to warm them.

"I have an apple here, too," he broke in. "It's really too much for me."

"No, thanks," she said, as she turned her body away from him, took her letter out of her purse and began to read it again.

"You don't have to turn away like that," he said, reassuring her. "I wasn't trying to read over your shoulder."

"No matter," she said, "it would be of no interest to you."

"You never know," he said, as he took a bite out of his apple.

"Never know what?" she asked.

"Never know what would be of interest to me. For one thing, if I may say so, that letter seems to be of great interest to you. You read it over several times just in these few minutes while sitting on this bench with me."

She folded the letter and put it back into her purse. "You are prying," she said, "and I find that very objectionable."

"Just verifying what I know of you from the hospital," he said. "I've seen your record."

"What record?"

"About your impersonating a nurse. It seems that it's been going on for a while now."

"Why would I deny being a nurse if I were impersonating one?"

"I could think of reasons," he said.

"I'd say you've got some problems, mister, in how you interpret things."

"I don't think so. Like I said, I'm a doctor."

"So you say. What department are you with?"

"Are you always this suspicious?" he asked.

She didn't answer him.

"Do you mind if I finish this, then?" he asked, holding up the remains of his apple. "I couldn't wait till you decided if you wanted it. Sorry." She stared ahead, not acknowledging him.

"I'll finish it then, if you don't mind." He took another bite, and then looked pointedly at her.

"That letter you were reading is from me, isn't it?"

"Well, it certainly is not," she said sharply. "Why in the world would I be getting a letter from you?"

"Well, I'm not sure I can recall just now why I might have written it, but it looked like my handwriting from what I could see of it. And it has my letterhead. I noticed that."

"It's the hospital's letterhead," she said flatly.

"Well, I can see why you might think that. They're all pretty similar." He smiled and studied his apple.

"What's in the letter then, if you wrote it?" she asked, without looking at him.

"I forget exactly. I write lots of letters. Doctors write lots of letters."

"You're no doctor," she said, now more softly. "And I'm sorry about this interchange. It need never have happened. I'm sorry for my part in it. I have to get back now."

"No, don't go just yet," he said. "I was only trying to help you."

"I don't see that you're helping me by asking me silly questions."

"Don't you remember me at all?" he asked.

"Remember you? What is there to remember?" she said.

"That you're my patient."

She stiffened and looked coldly at him: "That I really doubt," she said, then got up from the bench and walked in the direction of the hospital.

"Here, let me walk with you," he said softly, getting up and following a few steps behind her. "We could walk back together and some of the staff could remind you."

She stopped, turned to face him, and asked coldly, "Remind me of what?"

"That you're my patient here."

"I don't think so," she said, adding, "I'd appreciate it if you left me alone now," and walked briskly to the hospital entrance, looking back for an instant to see if he was still following her.

He wasn't.

He stood still and watched from a distance as she summoned one of the guards with a wave of her hand, said something to the guard, who then went up to him.

"Here, let me walk back with you," the guard said.

"Why?"

"No harm in walking along with you, sir, is there? I'll just walk along with you, if that's all right with you."

"Well, if you must," the man said.

Matilija Road

Jerry, our realtor, drove us up Matilija Road in Ojai to see Mr. Drew's house, which was for sale. We were looking for a low-priced second home in the Ojai area to which we could retreat on weekends. My wife wanted one that was not only inexpensive, but had a spiritual quality as well.

That's what had brought us here, to Matilija Road, which runs along a winding valley cut by Matilija Creek, with hills on either side heavily contoured as if by fresh upheavals, and outlined with the sharpness of a fairytale illustration.

Mr. Drew's house was one of fifty or so houses built on a mile-long ribbon of land running between the creek and the road, the lots divided by makeshift fencing idiosyncratic to each owner and typically built high enough to prevent being seen. The land itself was collectively owned by an association that had control over what was built or sold here.

Each lot was one to two hundred yards deep when the creek was low in late summer and a fraction of that when the creek was high after winter rains, the acreage misleadingly described as if constant, even when sporadically submerged.

The houses were owned individually by the association members but the land under them was owned collectively by the association. The houses were small, ramshackled, and depressing, but commanded extraordinary views of the surrounding hills, and sweetened by the air that flowed down from them. The people, too, who lived in these houses appeared worn and broken, strangely unrenewed by the surrounding beauty, like the dying patients in a mountain sanitarium.

Because of the fragile status of home ownership under the association, painstakingly spelled out in a thick founders document rivaling the philosophical justification of Christianity in complexity and believability, no bank would loan money on these houses. This could be a problem, our realtor said.

Another problem, too, was that Matilija Creek became a raging river with the winter rains. When the creek was low there was lots of land to look at and walk over. When the creek was high, though, the water was a menacing torrent at your door. There would probably be a year when all the houses were washed away unless the county reclaimed the area before that happened because of its being too unstable to service economically. The threat of endings was everywhere.

Matilija Road ended in a wildlife preserve, which the county also could not afford to maintain and had long abandoned doing so. Jerry, our realtor, was very candid about this, seemingly taking pleasure in noting what was wrong in buying there, pointing out that the road itself was strewn with rocks from daily landslides and often impassable during the year, and how that meant that you were in or out for longer than you may often want to be, and too frequently to be an adventure.

There was a yet more serious problem, Jerry reported, and that was that Mr. Drew did not want to leave the property after he'd sold it. He said he'd been there too long to leave, and had built a shack between the main house and the creek, which he had planned to live in after selling, saying that he was willing to adjust the selling price if the buyer would agree to this arrangement. Jerry couldn't suppress a smile as he told us.

The area seemed outside the ordinary world, both in its beauty and in what one had to give up to own a part of it. It had low value as real estate because neither nature nor the county nor the banks would commit to it. The bank's position also meant that the seller must carry the mortgage. So purchasing a home there forced some extra connections between buyer and seller that might not be welcome; in Mr. Drew's case it meant even more: It meant adopting him. Which was not simple. He was eighty-seven years old and almost totally blind. In addition, his shack was almost sure to be swept away if the creek rose to any appreciable level, which it could any winter now. I did not know of Mr. Drew's disaster plans but I assumed they were minimal.

Jerry was inclined to indirection, including his account of Mr. Drew, whom it turned out he had known for many years, and apparently did not like. Jerry would not say why, but remarked only that Mr. Drew did not recognize him. The implication was that Mr. Drew should have, but that his not doing so was not surprising.

Jerry also seemed remarkably casual in describing the property, pointing out its bad features. We had seen other properties with Jerry and he never appeared enthusiastic about any of them. I thought perhaps this was his particular approach to selling real estate: to pretend that he did not care if we bought anything or not.

His negative comments about Mr. Drew seemed to be of this type, as he continued to remind us of Mr. Drew's requirement that he be adopted.

"He'll be staying here with you, you know," Jerry said, waving his hand in the direction of the shack. "That's how it is here." In any case, it was becoming even clearer that Jerry did not like him, and walked on ahead with my wife, who seemed to share his view, thus leaving me pretty much alone with Mr. Drew.

And so it was when we went up to the main house. It looked homemade from manuals and pick-up help, and assembled over years. The main house was actually two separate living sections, a ground section and an upper section. The ground section was a one-story concrete block rectangle filled with old clothes and household articles as if camped in, with paint-spattered windows looking onto the surrounding hills. The upper section was a narrow two-story brick building with no windows, perched atop one end of the ground section and accessible only by walking across the roof of the ground section. It appeared that Mr. Drew was building his houses on top of each other, each narrower than the one beneath it which became its base, and having no architectural relationship to each other. He had apparently stopped at the second story of the upper section when his eyesight failed him.

My assessment of Mr. Drew's eccentricities grew as he proceeded to show us the interior of the upper two sections, which he said were occupied by a tenant. He motioned us to follow him across the roof of the ground section to the entry door of the first upper section, went up to the door, and began pounding on it, shouting that he wanted "to show the house to some people." Jerry and my wife stayed behind, safely at ground level, showing no sign whatever of intending to follow Mr. Drew. This left only me to accompany him, which I felt obligated to do. I hoped no one would answer his pounding and shouting. After a second vigorous pounding on the door by Mr. Drew and more shouting, the door slowly opened. He loudly announced his mission to the tenant, who had not yet appeared, at the same time motioning me to follow him in, which I did, albeit reluctantly, looking back to see if my wife and the realtor would be following me in, which they weren't.

The first thing I noticed when I stepped inside was the devastating heat. It was cool outside, but inside it felt well over 100 degrees. The heat carried heavy food smells laden with greases, suggesting the boiled bodies of animals. It reminded me of the hot, airless kitchen of my father's restaurant in Cleveland, with animal fats and lye boiling in huge pots to make soap, and of the slaughterhouse smells in Chicago where my grandmother lived. I became then aware of another pounding: this was the ponderous uneven footfall of an acutely distressed woman trudging up the stairs to the third level to get out of sight before we caught full view of her. I managed to catch a glimpse of her, disheveled and unkempt, seemingly scurrying to a deeper recess of her overheated burrow. I could hear her groaning as she made her way up the stairs and felt distressed with the inhumanity of our intrusion. I stared at Mr. Drew with bewilderment and could not believe that I had actually followed him in here.

At that point Mr. Drew appeared to me to be less than human. He reminded me of an extreme version of the cartoon character Mr. McGoo who would get into comic predicaments because of nearsightedness, except that this was not at all funny. The situation seemed grotesque and I was in the middle of it. It was as if a stranger had invited me to see something interesting and then proceeded to murder a wholly innocent person. My following Mr. Drew had made me an accomplice. My only thought was to get out of here. As I turned to do so, I heard Mr. Drew bellow, "Come and see this room too!" I looked back and saw that he was about to enter another room. I said, "No," but that only made him shout louder and more insistently. "Come and see this room too!" To quiet him I entered the room.

My sense of surroundings immediately took on a more distressing cast. There in the room we entered was a small boy, devastated by some crippling illness, half lying, half sitting in a cardboard box, unable to move or turn his head toward us, but apprehensively aware of our presence. Unlike the woman (whom I supposed to be his mother), the child could not escape. I felt wretchedly guilty—a beast of prey who surprised his helpless victims by invading their nest, catching them at their most vulnerable, the mother forced to abandon her crippled child to the predators. Mr. Drew instinctively pushed events to the macabre— he began bellowing good-natured greetings to the boy, which must have terrified him, since he could not turn his head toward us. I had a fleeting sense that we were killing the boy by this assault. It reminded me of frightening a pet canary in its cage when I was a child, causing it to bang itself half to death against the cage ribbing. This child could not even do that. Could not move in its cage. He was wholly at the mercy of the intruders, who, as far as he knew, had made his mother and sole protector abandon him to beings that were now wholly capable of destroying him.

I turned my gaze away from him to the other parts of this room. There I saw the artifacts of this little creature's wretched existence—an electric child's wheelchair and assorted apparatus needed for his care. I also became aware of a humming electronic sound like a machine for making audible speech. I had the sense that it had sputtered with some exclamatory sound as we had first entered, and that it had now fallen back to a flat state, like the heart monitors in hospitals that go flat when the patient dies.

I abruptly turned and left, going down the stairs with Mr. Drew following. There was little to say when I rejoined my wife and Jerry below, and waited with them as Mr. Drew came up to us.

He seemed winded and in some distress, resting his hands on his knees. "I'll help you get them out if you need me, too," he said. "Don't worry about a thing."

"Thanks," I said, and turned again to leave. As we walked off, we heard him shouting after us, "And don't you worry. None of us will be of any trouble to you."

Caretaking at the Andersons

E ddie noticed how the Andersons were looking him over, as if disapprovingly, and was surprised when they said at last that he'd do just fine. It was a short, uncomfortable interview in their living room, and Eddie was glad it was over.

They weren't comfortable people to begin with, yet the deal sounded pretty good to him. Eddie was a floater. In his mid-twenties, he had more or less odd-jobbed his way into different living situations. And this one seemed fairly attractive—a rent-free cottage in exchange for watering some oak and eucalyptus saplings and keeping their hillside property clear of weeds. Eddie had answered their ad and gone up for his interview.

Mrs. Anderson complained that the previous caretaker had not done well by them and that she was sure that Eddie would do better, that she could judge people, and that's why she decided that Eddie would do just fine. "Isn't that right, Jeffrey?" she said to Mr. Anderson, who nodded first to her and then to Eddie. She added that she and Mr. Anderson were Christian

Scientists and would Eddie have any trouble with that. He said, "no trouble at all" without being sure what it meant, but listened attentively as she went on. "We have to be careful about who we get up here, Eddie, can I call you that?"

"Sure," he said.

"The previous caretaker let everything pretty much die. Said he was watering everything, but he wasn't, was he, Jeffrey, not doing that at all?"

"No, Martha," Mr. Anderson said softly, leaning forward in his chair and nodding first to his wife and then to Eddie.

"Well, he wasn't watering like he was supposed to," she said. "Jeffrey here was supposed to check up on him, but he was way too lax with him. Mr. Anderson shrugged his shoulders and looked blankly at Eddie.

"Maybe it wasn't all Jeffrey's fault," she said, as if troubled at having embarrassed her husband in front of a stranger. "Jeffrey can't walk around well enough on the hillsides. I should have been checking on that caretaker myself." Mr. Anderson looked over at Eddie, sadly. Eddie nodded slightly to both of them, trying to show that he was listening but not taking sides. He began to wonder if the job of caretaking here wasn't for him.

"Well," she said, standing up, to show that the interview was over. "He had let all the oak saplings on the hillside die. They were so parched that their leaves had browned and curled. Any fool could have seen that. All of them pretty much dead. Over fifty of them. It broke my heart to see them." Eddie wasn't surprised to see her look over again in Mr. Anderson's direction. It was clear that Mr. Anderson wasn't off the hook, and Eddie began to worry that eventually she would also be dissatisfied with him.

As she walked him to the door, she said, "We've got the cottage fixed real nice for you." Eddie noticed that she had a way of pursing her lips when she finished saying something as if she'd said it just right and wanted you to reflect on it. "Jeffrey here will show it to you."

"Real nice!" Mr. Anderson chimed in, "I'll show it to you." He began to stand up, reach back for a cane that had been crooked over the arm of his chair, braced him with it, and finally stood, unsteadily. "It's this way," he said, motioning with his free hand for Eddie to follow him, maneuvering uncertainly around a coffee table near the door. "Arthritis," Mrs. Anderson broke in, and then sighed lightly as she watched him walk. "Arthritis," she repeated.

Eddie followed Mr. Anderson out the door as his wife closed it behind them. The man led Eddie down a narrow path to an overgrowth of weeds, which he tried to separate with his cane, almost falling into them from time to time, as Eddie held him by the arm to steady him.

"You don't have any lights out here?" Eddie asked.

"All burned out. The caretaker never replaced them. Be careful where you step."

Mr. Anderson stopped suddenly, turned toward Eddie, and peered past him at the light in the main house. "You don't see her in the window there, do you?" he asked. As Eddie said "No," Mr. Anderson reached into his pocket and retrieved a small flask.

"Whiskey," he said, as he unscrewed the cap and took a swill of it. "You don't mind, do you?" Eddie shook his head, whereupon Mr. Anderson added, "The old lady's a Christian Scientist. No drinking. No nothing, pretty much. No nothing." Eddie watched him take another swill, wondering if the cane was a prop, a way to account for his unsteady gait.

"Not much science to it really, Christian Science," Mr. Anderson exclaimed, "so far as I can see. More a religion, if you ask me. Anyway, whatever it is, it's OK with me. Mrs. Anderson is a good woman." Eddie could hear Mr. Anderson sigh when he'd said that, and felt sorry for him.

"It's right down the hill here, where you'll be staying." Eddie followed Mr. Anderson down to a dark end of the path to the door of a small cottage. Mr. Anderson must have known each step here, or he'd have long since fallen. "Here it is," Mr. Anderson announced, tapping his cane against it. He turned to face Eddie before going in. "I come out here when no one's using the place. To have a slug of this stuff." He tapped his pocket containing the flask, retrieved it, unscrewed the cap, and took a sip, after which he sighed audibly as if he had taken that sip just in time. "Want some?" he asked, waving the flask to Eddie.

Eddie shook his head. He didn't like the idea of taking this old man's sanctuary from him or worse, he didn't like the idea of the old man coming down here to visit Eddie and doing his drinking here. Mr. Anderson fumbled for a key in his other pocket. "Got it right here," he said, as if apologizing for taking so long to open the door.

"The old lady," he said, apparently short of breath now, from walking and talking and perhaps getting nervous about disclosing too much. "She's crazy with fear that somebody's going to get into this cottage, some drifter or something, and do something immoral." Mr. Anderson's voice trailed off as he finally got the door open and stepped in to turn on a light.

Eddie found himself standing with Mr. Anderson in a small, windowless room, a cot in one corner and a tiny bathroom with a shower stall in the other, a small bureau, a chair, a table with an oilcloth cover and a cup with a plastic flower in the center of it, a sink, toilet, and stove, and that was it.

"Not much, but it's home," Mr. Anderson said, stifling a laugh that turned into a coughing spasm. "Sorry," he said, walking over to the small bureau and opening the bottom drawer. "It's empty except for these," he said, bringing out a two-inch stack of magazines. The cover of the one on top was a photo of a naked young woman with her legs spread out. "Can't take these into the main house," he said with a stifled laugh that turned into another coughing spell, "so if you don't want them here with you, I'll have to burn or bury them or something."

"Just leave them," Eddie said. "I'll keep them for you. Don't worry about it."

Mr. Anderson looked hard at Eddie. "The old lady won't allow you to have lady visitors here, not overnight, if that's what you're fixing to do." He tapped his finger on the photo of the young woman, made a sour face and added, "It's her religion."

Mr. Anderson reached into his pocket for the flask and took another sip from it. "Sure you don't want any?"

Eddie shook his head and turned silent. Mr. Anderson eyed him suspiciously. "Sure you don't want any?" he asked again. "Let me ask you something then. Speaking of fixing, you're not fixing on turning me in, are you?" His voice was hard now, and he was shaking.

"No. What do you mean?" Eddie asked apprehensively.

"I mean you're not fixing on messing me up with the old lady, are you?"

"Why would I?"

"I don't know why you would or why you wouldn't. But if you did, I have a friend who'd make you regret it."

Eddie stared at Mr. Anderson, puzzled at what he was hearing.

"Don't worry about it," Eddie said, quite certain by now that he wouldn't be taking the caretaker job here.

"You're goddam right I won't be worrying about it."

Mr. Anderson hobbled to the open door and shouted loudly into the night, "Jack! You there?"

A figure stepped out of the bushes. Remarkably, Eddie had heard no sound of anyone being out there. It was as if this person had been standing there in the shadows outside the cottage waiting all this time for a call from Mr. Anderson.

It was a short burly man in coveralls, his forehead smudged with what looked like soot and wearing heavy workmen's gloves. He stood himself between Eddie and Mr. Anderson, fronting Eddie menacingly.

"You're not fixing on leaving the employ of the Andersons, are you, Sonny?" he said. "Fixing to leave them in the lurch."

"No," Eddie said, almost inaudibly.

"Because if you are, sonny, I'm going to personally see to it that you regret it."

"I'm not in employed here yet," Eddie said defensively, He felt Mr. Anderson standing uncomfortably close to him, and with the burly man so pointedly intimidating him, Eddie feared that anything, even a trifle, could set off this unstable pair.

"Now, see here, sonny," the burly man said, with a new clarity: "It's about you never even thinking about going to the missus, I mean, even thinking about turning old Jeffrey here in."

"Why would I do that?" Eddie exclaimed. "I'm not even planning on staying here." Eddie wondered if he should not have said that, that leaving might become an issue too. Also he shouldn't have made it sound like he knew what turning in Mr. Anderson even meant, which Eddie was not quite sure of anyway.

"Tell him, Jack, tell him." Mr. Anderson said, suddenly more animated.

"Sure, Jeffrey," the burly man muttered. "What I'm telling him is that his leaving before he started would be just as bad. That the old lady would suspect why he took off before he even moved in," then looking back at Eddie, and nodding in Mr. Anderson's direction, added, "She'd hold it against old Jeffrey here, so you see you got to stay. You can see that, can't you?"

"Yes, I can," Eddie, said weakly.

"Well, just to make sure you do, Jeffrey here and I are going to make sure you don't get it in your mind to leave."

"Yes, and just to make sure," Mr. Anderson chimed in, "Jack here fixed that door so that it can be unlocked only from the outside. Just till you get used to things."

Wally Jordan and the Guys at Gus's

I had just opened the bar at Gus's for my morning shift, some of the regulars following me in, taking their usual stools and ordering their usual drinks, followed by Joe Flaherty coming in to greet each of them by name and asking how things were going and listening to whatever re-tellings they chose to engage him in.

It was Joe's way, and they were all pleased to tell him about themselves.

And it was on this morning that Wally Jordan, one of Joe's favorites, had come in too and, instead of taking a stool near the others, took one at the end of the bar away from them. I went to ask him what he'd have and instead of ordering straight off, he leaned forward and muttered as if a secret, "I'm fucked."

Joe heard him and walked up to him to ask, as if he hadn't heard him, how things were going.

Joe had often told us how Wally had been an athlete once, world-class 440 runner as Joe told it, but even if true, what was visible now was only an old frame barely intact, a face boozed sour and eyes glazed from drink, what we saw wasn't exactly what Joe described, but the story he told took the place of it.

Wally was extra fidgety this morning, neither quite standing nor sitting, kind of half off the stool, unsettled and giving no hint to anyone of his next move. Wally was a jittery guy and of interest to the regulars in his own right, but with Joe's stories of him heightening it, whenever Wally came in, the regulars always took note of him.

Joe stood by Wally as he gulped his beer, shaking his head and muttering under his breath, "I lost her." He began to speak softly to Wally to settle him, asking him a question whose answer he probably already knew, "Who'd you lose, Wally?"

"Bernice," Wally answered, in a hushed, reverential tone as if speaking of a saint, then suddenly drawing himself up in a spasm of self-reproach, talked of how she had put up so long with his being a shit and forgiving him after each sin, cleansing him newly, but this was the end, she was leaving him now, had thrown him out, telling him she was done with him.

"That had to be really tough on you," Joe said, as Wally fell quiet and, putting his hand on Wally's shoulder, added, "Talk about it, Wally. It'll do you good."

Wally thought for an instant, then blurted out, "She found out about Maryanne," then choked on his words, asking Joe to fill me in. Joe turned to me, saying in his own words what Wally was suffering and, in my judgment, making a better story of it: "This was the Maryanne," Joe said, "who did Wally's nails, whose fingers trembled when they held his. He was getting his nails done twice a week because no one else trembled touching them, not even Bernice. It was like that," Joe said, looking over at Wally, who stifled a sob as Joe added, "That's what it was like for him."

I waited until Wally had settled down some before I asked, "How'd she find out, Wally? How did Bernice find out?" Wally tapped Joe on the shoulder and nodded for him to tell the rest for him.

"She saw them on TV," Joe said, "Wally and Maryanne. It was a one-in-a-million shot that she'd see them that way. How the hell could you figure a thing like that?"

Joe was the bar's expert on bad luck, especially on getting hit by a one-in-a-million shot, having seen them come up a lot. "You can't figure them," he said, taking up on Wally's tale for him, becoming even more clear that this was not the first Joe had heard of it, and continued. "Wally taking the nail girl to the Huntington pool, figuring it was nice to be there with a pretty girl, and feeling good about being there with her, not thinking in his wildest dreams that a local TV station would be there to shoot the whole thing—a Sunday special on the poolside crowd what with lots of footage on Wally and the nail girl too, and he didn't even know what was coming off, drunk in the heat of the afternoon and lying next to this steaming kid."

Joe shook his head, leaned across the bar to whisper to me. "This was the near final hit, this one just about doing Wally in," then turning to Wally as if checking if it was OK for him to tell the rest. Wally nodded, "Yeah, go ahead. Tell the hard part, Joe. You'd tell it better than me."

"Well," Joe continued, "Wally had told Bernice that he was sick, to forget their plans for picnicking, that he'd have to stay in bed all day, maybe a fever in him, not to bring soup, couldn't face that or anything, just too sick, he said, not expecting that in an hour or two that Bernice would be seeing him and the nail kid snuggling together on the side of the Huntington pool, and when he denied it, which was pretty dumb too, well, that was all it took, catching him two-timing and then lying, too—all too much for Bernice to see." Joe paused, took a sip of his beer, and muttered on Wally's behalf: "A million-to-one-shot, who could have figured it."

Joe talked a lot about the drinkers at Gus's and knew a lot about them because they felt comfortable talking to him, his talking softly and listening with soul, never holding court on his own, just sitting and listening to what anyone had to say, no one ever too drunk not to be worth Joe's listening to them, to have their story re-worked in Joe's mind to re-set it in the best light for telling.

Like when Wally would be near to passing out and draped over the bar like he was going to sleep, Joe would tell the rest of us not to wake him, that Wally was working on something tough, too complicated to work out sober, clear only when he was drunk, a way of thinking deserving our respect.

But what was or seemed to be ended abruptly when Wally disappeared. We hadn't seen him for a couple of months, and we all missed him, especially the regulars who asked Joe for news whom they supposed would have some if anyone did.

Then the mystery suddenly seemed to end as Joe came in one morning to say that Wally had sent word ahead that he'd be home and see us in Gus's soon, that he'd been on a job in Mexico.

Then nothing more for a couple of weeks, so we'd talk every day about what Wally might be doing if he wasn't dead, if he'd not already come back and taken up with Bernice, maybe she had taken him back, whatever, it made good talk. Joe was in the middle of it making suggestions about what might or might not be.

Then one day I got a call at the bar. It was Wally, "Don't say my name or anything," he said, "Is anything funny going on there?"

"Like what?" I said.

"Like is there anyone there looking for me?"

"None that I know of, Wally," I said.

"Well, do me one more thing. Take a look around the back parking lot and let me know what you see."

"Like what?" I asked.

"Just take a look," he said, "I'll hang on." I went out the back and saw some guys in a pick-up truck, just having a smoke, it seemed.

Getting back to the phone, "Nothing," I said, "Just some guys in a pick-up truck."

"Jesus," Wally said, "What did they look like?"

"Like Mexican field workers," I said. Then silence on the other end. "Wally, are you there?" I asked.

"Christ, don't say my name," I could hear him wheeze, "Don't tell anybody you talked to me."

"Sure, Wally," I said and hung up.

Joe sat near the phone and had heard enough to get the gist of it. "That was Wally, right?" he asked. "He called me last night. There's a contract out on him. Who could have figured that?"

When I told Joe about the pick up truck in the back lot, Joe went out to take a look for himself. "Yep, that's them," he said. "Those are the guys come to get Wally. They won't look for him inside, but figure that sooner or later he's going to come through that back lot where he parks, and they'll get him then."

This was serious. A contract out on Wally. With his bad timing he was dead. What could we do for him, maybe call the cops? The regulars had a thousand suggestions. "No," Joe said, "those guys will find Wally if they want. Wally's in real trouble here."

For my part, I didn't like the idea of guys lying in wait in our back lot to do one of our customers in. It would be bad for business to allow that sort of thing.

Joe seemed to know a lot more about it than he was letting on. So I wasn't surprised when he motioned me to come over so he could talk to me in private. He explained, "Wally went down to Ensenada on a sting to help bust a drug family for the local police, a family that everybody down there liked. Trouble was, so did Wally, so much so that he gets tied up with the drug boss's daughter, got caught up with his undercover role, becoming what he had only pretended to be because he couldn't help himself, especially since he felt on top of his game, with his timing coming back well enough to fool everybody, but it hurts him a lot when the bust goes down and everybody is arrested and the big shot's daughter is pissed. His story now is that the girl is the one who put out the contract on him. At first he feels good that he'd gotten his timing back and that he hadn't lost his looks, but now he's too scared to show up anywhere that they might be looking for him. Well, he pulled it off." Joe said, shaking his head. "Wally did!" Joe sounded proud of Wally, like he'd finally scored big. "The biggest con job of Wally's life," Joe said.

The next morning when I opened the bar, I checked out the back and saw that the guys in the pick up truck were gone. I waited for Wally's call to tell him the coast was clear, but he never called or showed up again. That was the last I or anyone else got anything direct from him.

To fill the void, Joe went over all the old stuff about Wally again and again till everyone at Gus's knew it by heart. All in all, Wally had gotten pretty famous at Gus's as Joe built him up, the guy who was once a regular like themselves and went out and made good.

Eddie and the Cashier

E ddie had thought about it all day, bacon and eggs for dinner at his favorite restaurant, only to be told that it would cost him an extra dollar. "There's a surcharge for ordering from the breakfast menu at dinnertime," the waitress said. Eddie felt that she was scolding him.

More the way she said it than what she said. It was that that bothered him. It was on his mind all through his dinner, so much so that he didn't enjoy eating it. When he finished, he fished in his pocket for a toothpick, put it between his lips then fished some change out of another pocket to leave as a tip. A small one tonight, and who could blame him. He didn't appreciate the waitress's attitude a bit.

Eddie followed her movements with his eyes as she waited on other tables. It seemed to him that she was friendlier with other customers there. She shouldn't have talked to him that way, like he was a stranger.

Eddie looked over at the cashier. She was very pretty and Eddie always liked looking at her. Always tried to get a table from where he had a good view of her. Of her long brown hair falling over her bare shoulders. He had a good view of her tonight.

That's why he took his time, working that toothpick. Took his time to leave, relax and enjoy himself, letting the waitress fret about when he was going to leave so she could clear his table. She shouldn't have talked to him like he was a stranger.

Eddie sat working the toothpick from one side of his mouth to the other, pausing every now and then to pick some last bit of his dinner from between his teeth, all the time his eyes on the cashier. She would see him watching her if she ever looked his way, which she didn't. He'd never really said anything ever to the cashier except "Here you are," when he'd go up to her counter to pay his bill. He probably was like furniture to her.

Maybe tonight he could get to know her better. Maybe ask her if he could buy a coffee for her. She wouldn't even have to leave her register. Just sip it in front of him while he talked to her.

Eddie finally got up to pay his bill, and placed it with a ten-dollar bill in front of the cashier as usual. "Here you are," he said.

It surprised him when she pushed it back to him. And even more surprised when she added, "You'll have to pay at the downtown restaurant. The breakfast register is there."

"Breakfast register?" he asked. "What downtown restaurant?" He thought at first that she was joking. He liked the idea that she might be joking with him, like he'd seen her do with other customers who would linger around the register laughing with her.

He stood smiling in front of her trying to look like he was going along with it, the joke, rolling his toothpick with his lips, working it from side to side and trying to twinkle his eyes to show her that he was going along with it.

Then she repeated what she'd just said without even looking at him, "You'll have to pay at the downtown restaurant. They have the breakfast register there."

"I don't understand," he said, to which she replied flatly, "You should have ordered from the dinner menu if going downtown is going to be such a problem for you."

The problem wasn't his, he felt. It was the restaurant's, for not keeping all their registers in one place. Eddie's first thought was to leave the money in front of the cashier and just walk out the door. It wouldn't be like he was leaving without paying. It would be that he just wasn't paying the way he was supposed to, a way he had no way of knowing about. But if he did he could never come back again and this was his favorite restaurant. Besides, he still wanted to be on the good side of the cashier. He hadn't given up on her.

And he was taking up too much of her time already. Too long thinking about what to do. He had to let her know right away whether he would go and pay downtown or whether he was going to cause a problem here. Eddie saw her glance toward the kitchen serving counter, and could see the head of the cook peering at him. Eddie had been coming here long enough to know that the cook peered out that way whenever there was trouble. Otherwise he'd stay out of sight, away from the serving counter, so you could see only his hands as he put orders up on it, or coming up to reach for the tumbler of whiskey he occasionally placed up there for convenience. Eddie knew about the cook's drinking.

He also knew that the cook was pretty sick, as he was coughing and wheezing all the time. Eddie figured the cook to have had his own score to settle with him as well, for when the waitress had ordered Eddie's bacon and eggs, the cook had yelled, "Tell him he can't. That's a breakfast item." The cook's yelling had caught Eddie by surprise and some of the other customers, too. And it must have cost the cook something to yell like that, for he had fallen back out of sight after doing so and into a renewed spasm of coughing and wheezing.

The cashier turned back to Eddie, and expanded on what was required of him. "It's downtown at the main restaurant. The breakfast register. This restaurant is just a satellite."

Eddie had never heard of such a thing. A satellite restaurant. He had been eating for a year at a satellite restaurant. It crossed his mind again to walk out without paying. They'd chase after him and be glad just to have him pay, even outside, on the sidewalk, after grappling with him. But of course he couldn't do that. He decided he'd have to go along with it, but it wasn't right.

Eddie realized that other customers had been overhearing this, for they were looking his way. Not only that, but the whole restaurant seemed quieter now than it had been. It seemed that even the clanking sound of silverware and dishes had stopped. "Alright," he said. "How do I get there?"

"By bus."

"By bus? I have a car parked right outside. I can drive there right now. Just tell me where it is. I don't need to go by bus."

"It's the only way we can accept. The bus is out in back. Better go out there now to get a seat. It'll take off as soon as we close. Don't forget to take your bill with you. They'll need to see it at the other end."

Eddie went out in back and was surprised to see that the bus was almost filled with other passengers. He wondered if they were all there for the same reason he was. He'd seen some of these passengers before at the restaurant. One had been arguing this very night with the cashier before Eddie had even gotten up to pay his bill. Maybe about the same thing as Eddie. He would have liked to talk to him, but the guy was sleeping now, and snoring so loudly that Eddie had to take a seat as far away from him as he could. Behind a family of four who'd gone out for the evening and had come onto the same problem too. One of the children, a little girl of about five, was grumbling that they were supposed to see a movie after dinner and had ended up on this bus instead. Eddie could tell from their conversation that it was because their mother had ordered pancakes.

Eddie was beginning to fall asleep under the sound of their voices and the little girl's crying, when he was awakened by the sound of someone having a coughing fit. It was the cook who had just come onto the bus. Eddie watched him get into the driver's seat and place what looked like a tumbler of whiskey on the floor by his feet. The cashier and waitress were on the bus too, sitting together in the seat behind the cook. Eddie guessed that the cashier would have to come to the downtown restaurant to ring up all these breakfast bills for food ordered that night and that the waitress might be needed to keep track of the customers who were bringing them, to make sure that none were missing.

Eddie must have dozed off, for the next thing he heard was someone announcing, "The downtown restaurant. We're here. They'll be calling us in soon." Eddie looked at his watch. He would ordinarily be in bed by now.

Looking through the bus window, he could see the cashier inside the restaurant turning the key in the register. She was opening it for accepting payments. And the waitress stood behind her with a packet of what looked like duplicate checks, one for each customer here, he supposed.

There was an air of excitement on the bus that they would soon be paying and be done with it. He watched along with the others for a few minutes as the staff got things ready inside. It seemed odd to Eddie that there were no customers here but soon realized that it was probably open at this hour just to take care of customers from the satellite restaurant who had ordered like he had.

Eddie was the last to get off the bus and joined the line at the end. Some others seemed to know their way around better than he. Eddie supposed that this might not have been their first experience with this.

Still, the line moved very slowly, there being some minor arguments with customers who were still not fully awake. When Eddie's turn finally came to pay, he put the check and a ten-dollar bill in front of the cashier and said, "Here you are," politely, as he always did. Even now, Eddie didn't want to say anything different from what he usually said when he paid. To his surprise, the cashier stiffened and pushed back what he had placed before her. "We can't make change at this restaurant at this late hour," she said. "You should have known better."

Eddie looked back at the bus and noticed that the others were for the most part already back on board, and the cashier, cook, and waitress were closing up and anxious to leave. "I've got to close up here," the cook wheezed, "and get these people back." The cook began to shake in the late night air and Eddie watched as the waitress led him to a corner of the restaurant and poured him a half tumbler of whiskey.

"Well, we can't leave you here," the cashier said, irritably, as Eddie was the last customer there. "We've got to take you back with us and bring you back tomorrow again after closing. I hope we'll have enough seats then. Be in the back of the restaurant after closing. And have correct change with you this time."

As they got on board, Eddie noticed that the other passengers were in a festive mood, singing and laughing and getting acquainted with each other. Except the waitress, cook and cashier, who took their seats without speaking to anyone. Eddie was the last to get on board and went to the rear to find a seat. The other passengers seemed to be relieved that this trip would soon be over. There was some talk about what each had ordered that had not been on the dinner menu. Eddie listened but did not say anything. Maybe on the bus trip tomorrow he would talk to others and share this experience with them. Not tonight, though. He wasn't ready.

Chinese Exhibit

T he girl helped me with the headphones and tape player.
The banner over her read: "Excavations from the tomb of
the First Emperor of China. See life-size earthenware warrior
figures and assorted animals of silver, gold, and jade, dating from
221 BC, all on exhibit."

The scent of hair spray was on the headphones, mixed
with the girl's deodorant as she drew the strap of the tape player
over my shoulder. "You push this little green button here to
start"—and with rising intonation, added—"and this little red one
here to stop." So softly patronizing for that instant. And then
abruptly she was done with me. "Through there," she said,
pointing to the first exhibit room. Blankly adding, "Enjoy."

I didn't want to go in yet—not without the tape set to
explain what I was seeing. I pushed a button. A soft voice said,
"And I so loved you." It had been a mistake. The button I'd

pushed was yellow, not green. The voice sounded a bit like that of the girl who had just helped me. I looked back at her. She was working with other patrons. I wondered if this was on all the tape players.

I let it play on without entering, to hear if her voice would return, but it did not. Only static...then what sounded like voices coming forward from a distant place—from far in the background, as if indistinct words of others had come onto her when she was recording this. One of these voices finally came forward, a different voice emerging from the background, announcing, "To return to the exhibit narrative, push the green button... *now*." I looked back at the girl again to see if that would be all right with her but couldn't catch her eye.

I pushed the green button. Only Chinese music on it. No exhibit narrative. No voice to explain what I was seeing, or would be, once I got in. I waited for the music to end, for some voice to tell me to enter. Maybe there was only music on the green button on my tape. Maybe mine was the only one with a green button like this one. And perhaps the only one with a yellow one too. I stood waiting for some sort of indication that I should go in.

Two women with shaved heads brushed past me and went in. They looked like they knew their way around this museum. Around all museums. As I watched them disappear into the first exhibit room, the girl who had helped me with the headphones came up to me. For an instant I thought it might be to ask if I'd heard her voice on the yellow button. But it was only that I was blocking the entrance to the exhibit room and would I please step back. No special signal about her being on my tape.

I stepped back and into an old man who almost fell over on me. Maybe not much older than me, but very unstable—tall and bent and with a great head like a horse—I thought of Picasso's agonized horse in *Guernica*. He had been just ahead of me in line for the tape players, flanked by two women who seemed to be in charge of him. There had been a bit of a row with the girl who had given them the tape players about who was going to help the old man on with his, the girl or one of his two caretakers. He was grumbling that he didn't want one anyway, that he wanted to go home. At the end they had prevailed on him to take them, forcibly cradling the headphones over his head and strapping his tape player to him. One of his caretakers pushed his green button and squeezed his hand reassuringly. I could hear him hissing through his teeth as I got fitted with my own.

All three of them came up to stand with me as if a foursome, all waiting at the entrance to the first exhibits room. At last, a new voice on my machine, telling me to go in. The voice was fully Western, promotional and reassuring, a voice from Disneyland, a voice from make-believe, from entertainment. I don't know what I expected—maybe Charlie Chan broken English—awkwardly transmitting ancient Chinese ways to Western temperaments.

The voice on tape said: "You are about to have a fascinating glimpse into two of the world's greatest empires and the ancient peoples who built them. Come see the objects that were discovered in what is considered to be one of the most significant archaeological finds of this century."

The old man and his two caretakers followed me in as if my going in was their cue to follow me. I looked over at the old man. He was pawing at the strap holding his tape player, very agitated now. He saw me looking over at him and began to shout at me. "It's Chinese music! All this goddam thing has on it is Chinese music." I looked away immediately, as he was shouting over the voice on my own tape and causing me to forget to move along as my own tape progressed, and losing my place in the narrative, the tape describing something I wasn't seeing. Maybe on the other side of the room. One of his caretakers pulled him over to the side and whispered something to him, prompting him to yell, "What?" very loudly. Apparently he couldn't hear her over his headphones. He was shouting over his Chinese music. I moved to the other side of the room.

There I found myself standing before a floor-to-ceiling map of modern China marking the territories of the early dynasties. I tried to read the card next to it when I realized that the tape I was listening to was describing an exhibit, not a wall map. I had made a wrong turn.

I looked to the other sides of the room—three exhibit cases, one on each of the three remaining walls. My tape must be synchronized to one of them. The old man and his caretakers right behind me. I was afraid that there would be more ruckus if he realized that what was being described had no relationship to what he was seeing. Sure enough, he did. And began yelling again.

I went to one of the three exhibit cases at random, hoping it was the right one and that the three weren't following me.

The tape said that I was looking at a horse that looked more like a dog to me. An early horse, I wondered, an early horse small and dog-like as perhaps they all were in those days. I recalled drawings of the presumed evolution of the horse from small non-horse-looking creatures to larger more horse-like ones. Maybe something to do with the ancient Chinese custom of binding young women's feet. This perhaps a young horse bound early to shape it into a dog-like form. I read the card in front of the exhibit case. It *was* a dog. I was out of synchrony.

I could hear the old man arguing with his caretakers from across the room. Then two more voices—male voices, authoritative and directive. It was two members of the museum security staff. Not effete types but two burly guys who ushered the old man and his caretakers out. As they passed, one of them gave me a harsh look. I was grateful finally to be freed of them and left to concentrate on synchronizing my movements with the tape.

I wandered into another room and chose an exhibit case in it at random. The card on it read that this was a bronze horse, while the tape was saying that it was a dog and warning me about taking any more wrong turns. "Look for a dog," it said.

I went back to the dog-like horse exhibit in the previous room whose card read that it was a dog. "Good," the tape said, "now go into the next room." That would be easy. There was only one next room. I found it full of people. Scarcely anywhere to stand. The voice went on to explain that before me (which I couldn't see, since I was pushed so far back) were twelve of the seven thousand life-size terracotta warrior figures that had been buried with the emperor along with all of his wives who had not borne children and all the workmen who had been working the last shift in the tomb. The voice had an upbeat positive tone, a Pirates-of-the-Caribbean discovery cadence, as it recounted how the workmen, among them no doubt some of the artisans whose works we were enjoying here, in no way wanting to join the dead emperor, had the surprise of their lives as they got entombed with him.

I pushed the red button to stop the tape till I could get through to see these figures mentioned in the museum brochure as the highlight of the exhibit. While waiting, I thought to press the yellow button again. "You're back," it whispered—the girl's voice again. She sounded exhausted. "It's too late," she said...static again...then distant sobbing, fading to sighs and then silence, except for the sound of wind, and the faint sound of hammers pounding chisels across stone, as in a cave, as in a tomb. Disney-type sound effects to convey the agonies of barren wives suffocating.

Drawing from the Figure

A n older man I was drawing as he ate had tried to take no notice of me, but a little boy, sitting with him did, who sat bolt upright in his chair straining to eat politely while staring at me. Postured so, it was easy for me to draw them. I raised my eyebrows in a "Do you mind?" look, slight and off-handed, almost beyond noticing, and scarcely caring if they did.

The boy caught it though and looked at the older man, and the older man then looked at me. Only for an instant yet long enough for me to capture his eyes, close set and blue to grey, and squinting, like the eyes of someone who had been at sea. A fisherman, I supposed, and I drew a cap on him.

"What's he doing, Poppa?" the boy asked, leaning across the table then looking back at me.

"Nothing," the older man said, glancing at me for an instant, long enough for me to capture those eyes again and set them even closer and now all but squinted shut, as he turned out what little blue I had seen in them.

"He's drawing you, Poppa," the boy said. "Can we see?"

"Finish your food, Danny," the older man said. "Finish your food so we can leave."

"But it's your face he's drawing, Poppa, it's your face and I want to see."

"No time for that," the older man said. "We've got to leave."

"I just want to see what the man's drawing, Poppa. I think it's you, and I want to see."

"Don't make your Poppa mad, Danny, by saying that again. What that man is drawing has nothing to do with me. Nothing to do with either of us, what he's doing there."

"No, Poppa, look. He's got colored pencils and everything, like we have at school. And he's drawing you, Poppa."

"Don't you be looking over there anymore, Danny," he said sharply. "Let him be."

"But I want to see what he's drawing of you, Poppa." And with that, the boy slid off his seat, walked around to the older man's side, studied his face to see what I had seen and fixed on there, then back at me. The boy's eyes, now settling on me, were wide set and brightly brown, like his mother's, I supposed, and I thought to draw them, too.

pulled him back to his seat, then whispered loudly, "You sit right down here, Danny, until you're through. Hear me clearly, Danny, you hear. Until you're through!"

I drew a thread of a line to separate the fisherman's lips, letting it droop at the corners to frame them.

"Poppa! Poppa!" the boy shrieked, freeing his wrist. "I've just got to see what he's drawing, Poppa. Don't you want to see?"

"Not another word, Danny!" he scowled, and for an instant cast a dark look at me, and I rubbed charcoal under his eyes to capture it.

Suddenly the older man shouted, "Tear that sonofabitch paper up, mister, or I'll do it for you!"

"I'm leaving in a minute, sir," I said, as I raised his upper lip slightly from his teeth, and streaked charcoal now across his cheeks. And his eyes, now set right, with all the color out of them.

"Well, then," the older man screamed, "I'll have to do it for you, won't I?" and made as if to come at me, but stopped as I knew he would, for he was a cripple and I studied him as he stood unsteadily at his table's edge, bracing himself on his crutches, for which I had left room on the paper to trace in.

"Yes, Poppa," the boy shouted, tugging at the older man's sleeve. "He's sure drawing you! Anytime you move or anything, he's drawing what you do! Anything you do, he does

Poppa!"

"Shut up, Danny," the older man growled. "What he's doing is nothing to me and should be nothing to you. Do you understand!" Menacingly, his body shaking, he waved one crutch at me, which I captured in a single stroke.

"I want to see what he's drawing of you, Poppa. That's all I want to do! Please, let me see that, Poppa!"

"Don't you talk back to me, Danny! When I say no, there's nothing more for you to say!" he shrieked, unfolded himself erect to stand as tall as he could, listed, and swung out at the boy with his crutch, losing his balance and striking the boy on the temple.

A fluttering smudge of charcoal was all it took, ending at the point of impact.

The older man fell to his knees, leaned over the boy and, putting his cheek to his, asked so softly in the boy's ear that I had to strain to hear: "Are you all right, Danny, sweet child?" he asked, but the boy did not answer. It was an instant that gave me what I needed, blending the common shadows that graced their cheeks.